I0656721

W. Knox Wigram

Five Hundred Pounds Reward

A novel. Vol. 3

W. Knox Wigram

Five Hundred Pounds Reward
A novel. Vol. 3

ISBN/EAN: 9783337245368

Printed in Europe, USA, Canada, Australia, Japan

Cover: Foto ©Andreas Hilbeck / pixelio.de

More available books at **www.hansebooks.com**

FIVE HUNDRED POUNDS REWARD.

A Novel.

BY A BARRISTER.

IN THREE VOLUMES.
VOL. III.

LONDON:
RICHARD BENTLEY, NEW BURLINGTON STREET.
1867.

FIVE HUNDRED POUNDS REWARD.

CHAPTER I.

LORD ST. MARGARETS' diplomacy had been really a success. He had had a difficult game to play, and had played it thoroughly to his liking. In the first place, with all his aversion to the alliance which his son was so anxious to thrust upon him, he had never allowed one syllable to escape his lips, which Ferdinand could by any possibility construe as exacting obedience, or indicating any unwillingness to let him follow up the object of his own choice. Lord St. Margarets had known perfectly well, from the beginning, that the match, for the time being, was out of the question. The Admiral, he was persuaded, would refuse his assent to any arrangement of the kind, so long as his pleasure required to be consulted at all. But that piece of information he had been careful to allow his son to acquire for himself. It was quite needless to urge what was absolute matter of fact, just as the sagacious engineer leaves the enemy to blunder upon a bonâ fide battery without warning, whilst he makes every possible parade of works which he would rather should not be attempted at all.

In the next place, his off-hand disparagement of Helen and her possessions, so careless and indirect as to appear like mere good-natured criticism, had its own time

and purpose. That it would have no immediate effect he was well aware. But it
would rest in his son's mind, 'nevertheless.
And when he found himself suddenly and
rudely thwarted at Riverwood, then was the
hour when it might be expected to bear its
fruit.

A man in the first bitterness of disappointment—one who has beheld his darling object
in life either vanishing altogether, beyond
reach and hope, or drifting silently ahead
into the shadowy and uncertain future, hates
to be comforted by those who would tell
him that the prize, after all, was nothing
worth. Why should people insult his judgment and mock his misery at the same
time? But, let him alone, and that is, probably, the very consolation which will ultimately spring up in his own mind. All
this had been foreseen by the thoughtful

father, who had scattered just sufficient en-
couragement for the soothing growth, whenever it spontaneously took place.

He was a little startled, certainly, shortly
after his arrival in Grosvenor Square, by
receiving a letter from Ferdinand dated
' The Queen's Prison,' and informing him of
all that had occurred. Not but that it
tickled him extremely, in one sense ; but he
felt vexed with his son for making such a
fool of himself, and considered that the Court
had been hasty, and taken a great liberty
into the bargain. However, he wrote a very
kind note in reply, informing Ferdinand that
he would take immediate steps to procure
his release, in order to get into any fresh
scrapes he thought proper.

What these ' immediate steps' were, you
will probably never know. Lord Chancellor
Bacon, they say, was open to arguments

more tangible than those employed in our
'windy war;' and his wink was as good as
his bond. No writer in a penny paper,
now-a-days, would hazard such imputation
upon even an imaginary judge—at least when
deciding between conflicting parties. But
Ferdinand's transgression might, in an in-
dulgent point of view, be looked upon as a
mere question of violated etiquette, and disposed of without vindictive displeasure. And
if his father couldn't arrange thus much,
why where would have been the use of being
Lord St. Margarets at all, and as good a
Conservative as the Chancellor?

In the meantime, having—in disregard
of Mr. Jacobs' friendly caution—so rapidly
succeeded in getting himself 'quodded for
nothing,' or rather for love, which in popular
phraseology means much the same thing,
Ferdinand had ample leisure to review his

own conduct, and find excuses, if he could, for what, considered in calmer moments, looked far too much like rash and reckless folly.

He would have given a great deal to have been able to undo much of the past, both upon Helen's account and his own. His father's solicitor could only inform him that his position was not one to be trifled with. He stood committed to prison in downright earnest, and during the pleasure of the Court. Beyond question, all intercourse with Miss Fleetlands must be suspended until that young lady attained twenty-one; and since it could serve no possible purpose to remain where he was, merely to indulge in the reflection that she was daily growing older, the sooner he made his submission, and took leave of the Borough Road, the better. The necessary steps should at once be taken. Probably the Chancellor might be disposed to view the case indulgently. It was just one of those matters which nobody could prophesy about.

Shortly afterwards, an intimation was received from the Lord Chancellor, directing that Ferdinand should attend at his private room in Lincoln's Inn, the following afternoon, at three o'clock. Thither he was escorted in a cab. Business was encroaching upon romance.

He was received with a degree of distant and freezing gravity, which might have chilled even the courage of a Victoria Cross. It was not until after some moments of saturnine silence, that his lordship condescended to appear aware of his presence, and ultimately to address him; and when he did, it was in a low, icy tone, and in syllables so far apart, that you might have counted them easily.

He was grieved, he said, and surprised, to see a person in Captain Hunsdon's high position, wantonly encountering the displeasure of the Court. For his conduct there could be no excuse. He had been warned, and had slighted the warning. He had disobeyed, and it was for the Court to weigh the circumstances of that act of disobedience, and inflict commensurate punishment. One consideration alone, induced him to stay his hand. Upon perusing certain papers before him, he perceived a statement to the effect that, in the event of his being discharged from custody, it was intended that Captain Hunsdon should at once leave England to join his regiment, then on foreign service. With a proper assurance to that effect, with a sufficient undertaking upon the part of Captain Hunsdon that he would thenceforth hold no communication whatever with the ward, until she should attain the age of twenty-one years—and upon Captain Hunsdon's making due submission, and paying all costs of his commitment, he was disposed to direct his discharge from custody. His lordship trusted that a warning so lenient, would neither be misconstrued nor forgotten. Captain Hunsdon might be removed.

There was nothing for it but to grin and knock under. Ferdinand would perhaps have been pleased to hear that, just before he entered the Chancellor's room, Admiral Mortlake had quitted it, after a ' wigging ' which would have astonished a midshipman, and for which he had been expressly summoned up to town.

The Lord Chancellor in fact had told him, in those peculiarly reassuring accents for which he was famous, that he considered his

conduct in allowing Helen to appear in the
hunting-field so insufficiently attended and
escorted, was a breach of his duty, grave
and scandalous; that out of regard for her,
whom the Court would presume to be innocent, he had directed the present proceedings
to take place in his private room; but that,
had it been otherwise, he should have
visited him with marked censure at the bar
of the Court. He warned him against supposing that he was himself the judge as to
who might be a proper match for his ward
—which it was for a higher intelligence
alone to determine; observed that he intended to consider at his leisure, whether
or not it was fit and proper that further
enquiries in the matter should be directed,
and concluded by pointedly desiring the
Admiral to observe, that what had already
befallen Helen, was nothing less than a

marked calamity, the result of most grievous negligence—and to pay all his own costs of the application.

After this benediction, the Admiral jumped into his cab, firing broadsides right and left all the way to the station. Even the ticket-porters themselves, those dreamy sentinels of the virgin apron and the pewter badge, who see a little of this sort of thing occasionally at the Court door, roused up sufficiently to nudge one another as he drove away.

Selfish people have at least one considerable pull over others, which need not be grudged them, considering that in most respects they are at no small disadvantage. Your thoroughly selfish man generally has the credit—to which most of us aspire—of knowing his own mind. Nothing conduces more to this sort of self-acquaintance than the caring very little what other people may feel, and not a bit in the world what they may think or say.   It was Admiral Mortlake's custom to make up his own mind, and then act upon his resolution as inflexibly as if he had only his late ship's company to deal with.

And it so happened that, just as Helen's little preparations were upon the point of completion, her guardian, one morning at breakfast, announced a plan which drove her either to put her project into execution without delay, or to consign it to indefinite postponement.

It had occurred to him, while smoking his afternoon pipe in the grim yew avenue, and meditating upon his late encounter with the keeper of Her Majesty's conscience, that a trip to the Continent would be the very thing under existing circumstances.   Helen had latterly begun to behave so very much better, that she deserved some reward. A month abroad—so, in his abysmal ignorance of the female heart, he imagined—would be quite sufficient to change the whole current of her thoughts, to fill her mind with new ideas, and cause all recent trouble to be regarded as a dream of the past. Paris cured most people, and a round home, through the pleasant roads of Normandy and Maine, would settle the business.

To tell the truth, he rather wanted to get out of the way himself. He couldn't think of Lincoln's Inn without choking. He had revenged himself, after his fashion, upon Lord St. Margarets, and found himself cut by the county. People, who had previously tolerated him as eccentric, now avoided him as cracked. Lord St. Margarets, indeed, secretly chuckling over the whole affair, lost

no opportunity of referring to it as an excellent joke, and declaring that it served
Ferdinand perfectly right, and would be the
best possible lesson to him against making
promiscuous acquaintances in future. But
this was not the popular view. Mortlake
could not even walk through the village
without being saluted by shrill cries of
" Cotched another Capting, guv'nor?" and
similar specimens of juvenile wit. Rough
allusions to himself and his behaviour were
chalked upon his park fence. Mr. Salterton's studied silence upon the subject was a
reproach in itself, whilst Sir Philip Chevy,
and young fellows of the Scatterley stamp,
threw all delicacy to the winds, and chaffed
him in a free and easy manner, which he
felt plainly enough, was intended to be in-
sulting. In short, he was in a very bad
position.

The proposition was a startling one to Helen. The idea of the Admiral, of all people, talking of going to France was almost too extraordinary to be credible. Under happier auspices, she might have been delighted with such a change; but the prospect of travelling in such company was not amusing, and she felt an irrepressible misgiving that the proposal was intended to cover some deep-laid scheme of which she herself was the object. A vague sense of insecurity tormented her. She felt that, once across the Channel, she would be perfectly in her Guardian's power, and the story of a month's trip might be really only a blind. Young ladies, who had been even less imprudent than herself, had been coaxed into convents, and expiated their incaution by lifelong imprisonment in a human menagerie. Was it possible that the Admiral had some intention of this kind, and proposed to return and take possession of her fortune, leaving her to the uncovenanted mercies of a Lady Superior? Vague and childish as were these alarms, they were sufficient to induce her, at any risk, to put her scheme of escape into immediate execution.

This was Monday. On Thursday the Admiral had proposed to leave Riverwood, and take the early train from St. Mark's to London. "Wednesday must be my day," thought Helen, and proceeded to remark how very pleasant it all would be, and to wonder when they might expect to find themselves in Paris.

Upon the whole this sudden arrangement seemed rather in her favour. Her plans were already matured; her summer-house-hidden disguise complete; and the bustle of preparation would probably render her task all the more easy. Nor was it without a sensation of mischievous delight that she reflected upon the strange consternation which would follow her sudden and inexplicable disappearance at such an unlucky moment; and upon the fine unpacking which would have to take place in the morning.

Wednesday arrived at last; and although, to do Helen justice, she had never for one moment wavered in her determination, or allowed her mind to flinch from the enterprise, it must be confessed that, as the hour drew near, her excitement became almost uncontrollable. She had determined to get away, if possible, about half past five o'clock, which would enable her to reach the railway station shortly after sunset; but, as the story of her travels belongs to another department of these pages, I shall at present say no more of her movements than is absolutely necessary.   Fortunately for her, the house was in that outrageous state of bustle and disorder which commonly precedes a journey upon the part of people altogether new to road and rail, and which is so highly amusing to seasoned old stagers like ourselves.   Still more fortunately, Mr. Salterton happened to be just then absent, upon a month's holiday. To have taken leave of him under the circumstances would have been more than embarrassing to Helen.   It would have been impossible.

She had, as you may imagine, been at Mrs. Mortlake's beck and call during the whole of the forenoon.   The good lady hated the projected journey more than can be told; and what with providing against every possible contingency, and anticipating every conceivable disaster, gave one the idea of a person booked for the moon, and laying in travelling-stock at short notice by the light of nature. In fact, Helen was called away from an agonising discussion as to the best method of economising space, as presented in the empty skull of a huge imperial, by a summons from her Guardian to his study below.

She had been sent for to rummage among the book-shelves for an old road-book, or ' itinerary,' of Northern France, which he had some idea would be of use to them in their expedition. But, whilst spending a good deal of time upon her knees to no purpose, the front door bell suddenly rang, and ' Mr. Clover and Mr. Twick,' were announced as visitors.

" Don't go," said the Admiral sharply, as Helen rose to leave the room. " Find the book first, at all events, or we shall start without it to a certainty. Ha ! Good evening, Clover. I am happy to see you, Mr. Twick."

It was evident that business of some sort was about to be transacted, for a broad new parchment deed, crackling like a bonfire, was unfolded by Mr. Twick, and the Admiral produced a bundle of brown documents upon his part from the recesses of the iron Ark. And then, biscuits and sherry were rung for, and an animated conversation took place, the purport of which was not clear to Helen.

"Three thousand pounds, we make the mortgage debt," began Mr. Twick, a jolly-looking, chestnut-coloured man of five-and-forty, with a curly head. "And half a year's interest, less income-tax, is seventy-three, two, six. You had a fancy, sir, Clover tells me, for the money in cash—so I've brought you three thousand-pounders.

Not every day one has the chance of hand-
ling a thousand-pound note.   Pretty paper,
isn't it?"

"Ha, ha!" growled the Admiral.   "You've
had your laugh against me, as you came
along, I'll be bound.   But money is money,
Mr. Twick, and if you'd lost what I've lost
by trusting to banks and clerks and all that
sort of humbug, you'd do as I do—keep a
strong box of your own.   Give you a week
to see your way through *that* door," added
he, glancing over his shoulder at the Ark.
"Now you want a receipt, I suppose, ha?"

" And your execution of this reconveyance,
please," replied Mr. Twick, spreading his
deed upon the table ; "and then Clover and
I will look over my client's documents together.   This is the parcel?"

"Those are the deeds, sir, as I received
them.   Probably you will attest my signa-

ture. I deliver this as my act and deed. Is all square, sir, ha?"

"All right, sir." And the Admiral, after having carefully scanned the three thousand-pound notes, and compared their numbers with a list handed to him by Mr. Twick, enclosed them in a great red leather pocket-book; and, placing it upon one of the iron shelves of the Ark, shut the door with a bang which made the room shake.

"Safe investment," observed Mr. Clover, with a slimy smile.

"So I fancy, at all events," returned the Admiral dryly. "For the present, at least. I have been advised to give matters a few weeks turn before making the reinvestment which I purpose. Things are going down in the city."

"There was a wonderful safe, shown at the exhibition of '62, by a man from Cork," remarked Mr. Twick, sorting his papers.

" You should have seen it, Admiral. You locked the door, and then dropped the keys into a little slit in the lid, which shut up of itself—snap! and there you were, safe as a church."

" How the devil did you get it open again?" inquired Mr. Clover, without taking his eyes off the table. Mr. Clover was a stubborn man of business, and beyond a joke.

" Ah! that's just what lost him a medal. The jury asked the very same question. Unlucky, wasn't it?"

" Can you and Clover stay and drink a bottle of port?" interposed the Admiral. " We dine at seven."

" Thank you, impossible! I have to be in London again to-night. Directly I've looked over these deeds of my client's with Clover, I must be off to St. Marks, and catch the six o'clock up train, if I can."

"Sorry for it. You shall give me a cast to St. Marks in your carriage, if you will. I have a matter to attend to there, which I quite forgot this morning. We are off to the Continent, all of us, to-morrow. Helen, tell Mrs. Mortlake where I've gone, and ask her to put off dinner. I shall be back by half-past seven to a second."

This was all in Helen's favour. Her guardian would be out of the way, which was one good thing; while, by suppressing the message to his wife, a great deal of bewilderment and mystification would be introduced at the critical moment, which was still better. For the Admiral was a rigidly punctual man in the matter of his meals. All sailors are so by habit. And to find him missing at dinner-time, would be almost enough to throw her own disappearance into the shade, and make his wife believe that chaos was come again.

The examination of the papers lasted some quarter of an hour, during which the Admiral retired into an adjoining dressing-room to change his coat. At last the documents were pronounced satisfactory, and stuffed by Mr. Twick into his great black leather bag. Another glass of sherry was filled all round to clinch the business, and in two minutes more the post-chaise was clattering through the lodge gates.

Helen looked at her watch. It was twenty minutes past five. "Now or never!" thought she, and was just leaving the room, when a sudden idea struck her. It was one of those presentient impulses which have occurred to most of us at some period of our lives, and of which it is impossible to give any reasonable account. She walked straight into her guardian's dressing-room, and examined the coat which he had just taken off.

A jingle in the breast-pocket, in which she had observed him deposit the keys of the Ark, rewarded her curiosity. They were actually there! clean forgotten, and left behind! O, man of Cork, you should have had this tale to tell, when the jurors waxed so foolishly funny over your invincible strong box.

With light, deliberate step, Helen proceeded to the Ark, unlocked it, and put the red leather book into her dress-pocket. She then refastened the door, replaced the keys exactly where she had found them, gave one glance round the room, and was gone.

I don't know that I am bound to account for every action which I may happen to have to record. What on earth could have possessed her, if I may be allowed the vulgarism, to carry off these bank-notes, passes my comprehension altogether. Whether it was a mild access of kleptomania—which, however, is commonly supposed to molest ladies under circumstances to which she had no pretension; whether she indistinctly fancied that she was securing a 'material guarantee' for the restoration of thus much of her fortune, at all events; whether it was sheer mischief, such as prompts the Gazza Ladra to make away with silver spoons, which are useless and out of place in her rubbishy nest, I have not the smallest idea. My conjecture, were I bound to conjecture at all, would be, that she was simply bent upon making the greatest row possible, and forcing on, at all hazards, a general explanation. Felony was certainly a strong measure; but a young lady who has been wronged, and is bent upon righting herself, is not apt to stick at trifles.

Certainly, if she could only have been

invisibly present at Riverwood that evening, her satisfaction ought to have been unbounded.

She had been missed, almost immediately after her departure, by the ever-watchful Crimp, who lost no time in informing Mrs. Mortlake of her suspicions.

For a long time, that lady was perfectly incredulous, and stubbornly refused to see anything remarkable in the story. Miss Fleetlands was somewhere about the place, she was certain—perhaps in the shrubbery, the garden, or the stables, and would reappear in due time. Crimp was talking nonsense!

But when another half-hour had passed away, and Helen was still unaccounted for, she was obliged to confess that it was a strange business altogether. A rigid examination of her bed-room, only made matters

more perplexing than ever. There was her
trunk, half packed, just as Crimp had left it
in the morning. Her toilet-table was exactly as usual. Not one single article—
even so much as a brush or comb—had been
removed. Not one iota of wearing apparel
was missing from its proper place. That
she had run away, seemed out of the question. Run away, without anything but
what she actually carried upon her back!
But where in the world could she be?

"May have made away with herself, you
see, mum," suggested Crimp, adopting an
explanation of absence which always sug-
gests itself to waiting-maids. "My Aunt's
mother, mum, drownded herself, fourteen years
come Michaelmas, with nothing on but a
strong calico chemise; and she having to
walk four miles, too, to get to the water;
and, what's more, was carried eleven miles

down stream before she was swallowed up—
leastways, it was that distance before she
was hooked out of the river by a strange
gentleman in a morning punt, if you'll be-
leive me, mum, and she not able to swim no
more than me, which is the most amazing
and fabulous part of it all."

"Nonsense!" replied her mistress. "Ladies
don't make away with themselves."

" Then she may be pursuing of her Captain, mum, in a po-chay and pair, which, to
my mind, she is morally doing at this solemn
moment."

As Captain Hunsdon happened to be just
then in the very middle of the Bay of
Biscay, this supplementary suggestion was
repressed with equal brevity.

" I wish your master were at home,"
groaned Mrs. Mortlake. " I wonder what
keeps him out, on this particular evening !"

"Lassy me, mum! Well, I thought of course you knew. The Admiral, mum, set out of his own accord, an hour ago or more, in a glass coach, with two lawyers—lawyer Clover and another, and drove right away down the St. Mark's Road. Quite fearful fast they went, mum."

Mrs. Mortlake started at the news. Not of course that she supposed he had eloped himself, and smuggled off Helen, disguised as a couple of solicitors; but his going without leaving word appeared exceedingly strange, and things seemed to be tumbling into confusion around her, like the difficulties of a dream.

"I cannot understand it," she gasped at last, subsiding into an arm-chair. "Crimp, let nobody in the house suppose that Miss Helen is not in her room. Go about exactly as usual. The Admiral will certainly be home by dinner time. He will know what to do. At least I hope so !"

But when dinner time arrived and passed, and the Admiral was as scarce as his ward, she really felt that if the floor were to open under her it would be more vexatious than surprising in such a bewildering *bouleverse-ment*.

Her husband returned at last, and entered his study alone, by the garden door. He had already missed his precious keys, and was annoyed to the last degree at his own carelessness. Hastily lighting a candle, he plunged into his dressing-room, and was gratified by hearing their clink in his coat pocket. To unlock the Ark, and ascertain that all was secure, was the work of a second. Imagine, if you can, his blast of rage and execration at the sight of the empty shelf ! It was something too terrible for description. His face turned absolute indigo; and if he hadn't torn open his necktie, to let the oaths out, he would certainly have burst upon the spot. Who the thief could have been he couldn't form the slightest conjecture; but O my goodness, if he could only have caught him, then and there!

"Gone—gone, ma'am!" he shouted, as his wife came hurrying into the room. "Gone, since I left home, not two hours ago!"

"Isn't it dreadful?" exclaimed Mrs. Mortlake, thinking, of course, that he referred to Helen. "What in the world will become of us? Where did you see her last?"

"In this confounded safe, ma'am; locked up with this infernal key! I left it in my pocket, like a fool as I am, when I went across to St. Mark's—and look there!" pointing to the empty shelf.

"Why, surely you never locked her up there when you went out!" cried the lady, looking horrified in her turn. "What an awful thing to do!"

"Of course I did! What else do you suppose safes are made for? And why the plague do you keep on calling it 'her,' like a Welch woman?" retorted the Admiral, thundering with rage.

"I'm talking of Helen!" shrieked the lady.

"And I'm talking of a red leather pocket-book, with three thousand-pound notes in it! What about Helen? She's not gone too— is she?"

A vigorous explanation followed, during which each party endeavoured to throw the blame of the young lady's disappearance upon the other, with the result usual in such cases. The mystery of the pocket-book was however cleared up at once. It was morally certain that Helen must have taken it, and almost equally so that it would some day or other be accounted for. Indeed the Admiral leaned to the belief that she had only removed it out of sheer mischief, and hidden it somewhere about the place,—not a very welcome piece of pleasantry, by the bye, considering its contents.

As regarded Helen herself, he at once formed a conjecture, which, although incorrect in fact, was plausible enough at the time. He fancied that some deep-laid scheme, at the instigation of Captain Hunsdon, was at the bottom of the whole affair. Somebody had driven by in a carriage, according to previous arrangement, and picked Helen up; whilst, probably through some misunderstanding as to the time, or in the confusion of the moment, she had been unable to make the slightest preparation for her journey. That, he fancied, would account for what was otherwise inexplicable, and instantly addressed himself to active measures.

Applauding Mrs. Mortlake for her previous discretion, and desiring her upon no account to allow the truth to be known in the house, but to say that Miss Fleetlands had gone to bed with a severe headache, and was to be kept quiet, as the only chance of being able to start in the morning, he sent a servant off at once, to procure the immediate re-attendance of Mr. Clover. In his note to that gentleman, he desired him to telegraph to London for a couple of detectives from Scotland Yard. In the mean time slops and dry toast were ordered upstairs for Helen, and the secret was kept with entire success.

As may well be supposed, the conference between the Admiral and his solicitor, when the latter arrived about ten, was long and anxious.

The predicament of the Chancery guardian of a run-away ward is never a nice one ; for the Court is apt to be horribly inquisitive in such cases, and to overhaul the unlucky custodian with a degree of acrimony which it would be difficult to exaggerate. In the present instance the Admiral, who had no mind for another excursion to Lincoln's Inn, had determined upon one desperate course of proceeding—not, as his legal adviser warned him, free from very serious risk, but still offering some chance of preserving Helen's name from the greatest possible scandal, and allowing her guardian, at the same time, to creep undetected out of a most awkward scrape.

If, by any ingenuity, the servants could be so far imposed upon as to believe that the morrow's journey took place with Helen in company, the story of her indiscretion might possibly be concealed altogether. The detectives and Mr. Clover could obviously do their work just as well, during the Admiral's absence, as if he were present at Riverwood ; whilst to break off the journey at the last moment, would be simply to invite everybody's curiosity, and probably ensure the discovery of the truth within twenty-four hours. In the mean time, should Helen be recaptured, she could be quietly conveyed to London, and her guardian telegraphed for at anymoment. Nothing compromising need ever transpire; and they must all take better care for the future.

Such was the plan of operations which it was ultimately determined to adopt. The two advertisements, which you may recollect already to have read, were at the same time sketched out by the Admiral, and 'settled' by Mr. Clover.

The first, you will remember, had reference to the bank-notes. The amount represented by these securities was far too large to be trifled with. Whatever might have become of the pocket-book, its restoration was well worth the one hundred and fifty pounds offered, irrespective of the fact that, if recovered at all, it might not improbably lead to some trace of Helen herself. The story of its having been lost upon the highroad was merely a fable, intended to make matters easy, should it ever happen to turn up.

The second, and descriptive, advertisement, which had so serious an effect upon poor Petersfeld, it was arranged should be suppressed until the detectives had had a fair run. Guarded as its terms intentionally were, they could scarcely fail to excite an undesirable amount of general curiosity. Besides, although the Admiral would at the moment readily have paid down five hun. dred pounds, were that the only condition of having his ward safely back again, he winced exceedingly at the notion of handing over such a sum, so long as there was the faintest hope of obtaining his object at a less ruinous rate.

Nothing at present remains, but to describe the device by which the household were to be deluded into the belief that Helen was actually of the party next morning. It was the joint invention of Mrs. Mortlake and her maid, and as a specimen of what very superfine people might stigmatise as low cunning, may be recorded.

Crimp, for her own part, undertook to leave Helen's room in such a state that no housemaid alive would suspect that she had not slept and bathed as usual. And in the meantime she carried so many messages down-stairs from Miss Helen, that although to serve her was the delight of the servants'-hall, people began to think her exacting.

In the next place, a half-length figure, composed of air-cushions, travelling-wraps, and the like, was dressed up in Helen's hat and burnous in the Admiral's room.

When the carriage was at the door, and after Helen's trunk had been ostentatiously corded in the hall, it was easy enough to get the servants out of the way, while her bed-room door was thrown open, and the figure handed by Mrs. Mortlake and her maid into the further corner of the carriage, instantly followed by the lady; the Admiral engaging the coachman's attention upon the opposite side. The transaction, taking place under the carriage portico, could not be criticised from the windows, which was an advantage. In short, nothing could have been more successful.

Nobody had the slightest suspicion—as how should they? Tricks like these are easily played when no one is upon the alert, or concerned in detecting them. Otherwise, you may deceive children and white mice, but not the fellow-creatures who live under your dining-room. What you know, they know : make up your mind to that.

During the drive to St. Mark's, Helen's effigy was quietly dismantled; and, whilst the Admiral talked to the driver, Mrs. Mortlake and Crimp walked into the station.

That coachman, honest fellow, could and would have sworn, had need been, that he had driven a gentleman, two ladies, and a maid to the railway-station upon that especial Thursday. Every servant at River-wood would have abetted him in his involuntary perjury, and not only pledged his or her oath to the effect that Helen accompanied their master and mistress, but sworn that they saw her in the carriage. So much for human testimony.

It had been arranged that they should arrive at St. Mark's a little before the train started, in order to give the Admiral time for a flying interview with Mr. Clover. In that gentleman's office he found the two detectives, just arrived from London, looking as like conjurers as they could, and asking questions with rich gravity—like medical men. And here let me assure you that you will hear no more of these worthies. I never yet encountered a detective in a story

who was not about as much like the original
as an average Englishman is to the John
Bull of a Paris novelist. I declare that
sooner than meet with such a character in a
friend's book, I would find one under my
own bed.

It was then settled, for reasons hinted at
in the outset, that instead of inserting the
names of Mr. Clover's London agents—
Messrs. Talbot and Castle, in the advertisement, Mr. Bloss should be the person to
receive applications, and pay the reward, if
claimed.

It was Mr. Bloss, if you remember, who,
a great many years ago, prepared the will
which made Colonel Fleetlands a millionaire;
—who wrote, upon old Nettleby's death, to
apprise him of his good fortune; and who
had actually received Helen herself at
Southampton, upon her first landing in

England. Naturally, as Nettleby's solicitor, he had been concerned with Talbot and Castle in the administration of the estate, and seemed the fittest person to fix upon for the above purpose.

It was hastily arranged, at the same time, that the Mortlakes should, by every means in their power, while abroad, keep up the delusion that Helen was in their company. It would be as well, for instance, always to keep a room in her name at hotels—write messages home in which she should be mentioned, &c., &c. But there was then no leisure for details.

And so, while the flag waves, and the whistle screams, and the train glides from the platform, let us allow the curtain to descend upon the Second Act of our drama.

CHAPTER II.

I DON'T mind telling you that this is the first time I ever found myself in the thick of a big story, like the present. It has grown, in the telling, to a length which I never intended, and, like certain unruly plants, may not have grown quite as straight as I could wish. When I undertook, some Chapters back, to make all square, by bringing my account of Helen down to the time at which Petersfeld thought fit to set out in pursuit of her, I little expected to drift away down stream, till our friend, and all belonging to him, dropped clean out of sight. No

matter now. What is writ is writ: and
critics must live. Let us, however, return
for one moment to the Albany.

We left Petersfeld, if you recollect, in
about the most dismal pickle in which a man
could well find himself. Dunned by his
tailor, without a penny to pay, and accepted
by a young lady to whom he had never proposed, there was only one thing to be done.

Tearing Mr. Bags' letter and Linda's
delicate little note severally into a thousand
pieces, and confounding the writers with
fierce impartiality, he hastily packed his
portmanteau, sent for a Hansom, and set off
at once for St. Marks'-on-the-Sea. It was
a pleasant place to stay at. Mr. Maldon
and his wife were civil and sociable ; and,
now that it was clear that Miss Fleetlands had not travelled with her friends to
the Continent, there was no reason why he

should not resume his search in good earnest. The inveterate dislike which all young Englishmen feel to being baffled, awoke with fresh force in his mind; and he vowed that, this time, it should go hard, but he would succeed.

You may have forgotten, and are forgiven if you have, that I myself, John Worsley, so far from being a mere narrator of other people's deeds, am an actor upon the boards. Indeed, now I think of it, I don't see why I should not have made a good deal more of my own part from the very beginning. There is, however, no help for it now.

On my return from the country-house where I had been spending my Easter Vacation, I lost no time in calling at Paul's chambers in the Albany, to hear, if possible, the latest news of his adventures.

But I found his outer door closed, and at

the entrance-lodge, I got no further information than that Mr. Petersfeld had left
some days previously, in a Hansom, saying
that he was going abroad.

Returning to Lincoln's Inn, the first person I chanced to encounter, in crossing New
Square, was Mr. Buttermere himself, in his
wig and gown. Directly he saw me, he
shouted rather than called, "Worsley—
Worsley! I want to see you at my chambers, immediately, if you please!"

He had just come out of court, and was
evidently desperately busy, with more than
one consultation-party waiting for him in
his ante-room. But he snubbed his clerk
for reminding him of the fact, with a fiery
brusquerie which was quite alarming, and
bidding him get the gentlemen to wait, led
the way into his own room, and desired me
to take a seat.

"Now, Worsley," he began, flinging his wig upon the table, "I want to know what has become of your friend Petersfeld."

"Unfortunately, that is just the question which I am unable to answer. I have this moment called at his rooms in the Albany, and found them closed. The porters tell me that he left, saying he was going abroad, some days ago. Beyond that, I know nothing whatever of his movements. As to where he may be at present, I have not even a conjecture."

"Went abroad!" exclaimed Mr. Buttermere, who was fast losing his temper. "That's exactly what I was told myself. Worsley, do you mean to pledge me your honour, as a gentleman, that you don't know where he is?"

"I have already told you all I know on the subject," returned I. "I suppose you do not require me to pledge my honour to that statement?"

"But, confound you!—I beg your pardon, I mean, confound him—I thought you lived together. At all events, you told me so, and you came to my house one night to dinner together. Worsley, you see that I am annoyed, very seriously annoyed, indeed. Here's this young fellow been making all sorts of love to my youngest daughter—Linda, you know—and sent her all manner of letters and presents besides; and now, in one moment, I'm to be told he's gone abroad! Gone abroad, indeed! without a word to her or to me, or to any of us. Of course the poor child is terribly cut up. That infernal Mrs. Springletop has been spreading the news of her engagement all over London, and boasting that she managed it all. I only wish to Heaven that something unholy would fly

away with her! Gone abroad, indeed!
This won't do, you know?"

I had never suspected that the smooth,
creamy tones peculiar to Mr. Buttermere,
could have been exchanged for accents so
ferocious, or capable of a clinching male-
diction, which it would be irregular to produce in print.

"I am quite certain," I replied, after a
moment's pause, "that my friend Petersfeld
is perfectly incapable of trifling with the
affections of any young lady. That he
should have done so in the case of your
daughter, whom he met at your own table,
is, to me, simply incredible. Of course I
am not going to suggest an explanation in
his absence. But that you have mistaken
his conduct altogether, and are bringing a
very needless charge against him, I would
stake my existence. I am satisfied that

when he turns up—as he is certain to do before long—he will be able to justify himself."

"Satisfied, indeed! It is I who have to be satisfied; and as to justification, he shall justify himself, by George! or I'll know the reason why! Worsley, I now give you a message for him personally, and I call upon you to deliver it."

"Mr. Buttermere, nothing has ever passed between us to warrant you in making me your messenger in this peremptory manner. If you like to entrust any communication to me, I will convey it to Petersfeld next time I see him. If not, you will probably allow me to withdraw from an unpleasant conversation, respecting matters with which I have nothing whatever to do."

For a minute at least Buttermere looked at me with a steady mistrustful gaze, drawing his hand slowly over his chin. Then he took a sheet of note-paper from the stand before him, and began to write. Then he suddenly stopped short, and offering his hand, said :

" Worsley, you must excuse me. I have behaved confoundedly ill. But Linda was my pet—my darling. Worsley, what I have to say can equally well go by the post. Good-bye. I am sorry that you should have seen me make such a fool of myself."

There was something to me inexpressibly touching in the emotion of my old friend, whom I had always regarded as the very impersonation of easy and unchangeable good humour. Alas, there is in this world —as Lambro, that famous sea-solicitor discovered in his day—many

" A deep grief,
Beyond a single gentleman's belief."

Especially among people who have daughters to marry.

"If you will send your letter to our chambers, Mr. Buttermere," I rejoined, "you may depend upon it that Petersfeld shall receive it within an hour after I meet him in town. In any event, the moment I ascertain his whereabouts, he shall be informed that it is awaiting him, and demands his instant attention. Good-bye, sir."

"Good-bye, Worsley. Will you tell my clerk as you pass, that I am disengaged, and desire him to show in the first consultation? Good-bye."

It occurred to me, before I reached Stone Buildings, that there was at least a possibility of Paul's beating up his old quarters, at the St. Mark's Bay Hotel. In short, it seemed so far from unlikely, that I wrote him a short note there, mentioning in a few words, the subject of the interview which I had just held, as well as the letter which awaited him, and strongly advising him to return to London at once.

In point of fact, as you already know, Petersfeld, so far from having gone abroad, was all this time indulging himself in eco-nomical retirement at that sequestered watering-place, little suspecting the trouble which he was giving his friends.

He found his good-natured host and hostess, Mr. and Mrs. Maldon, in excellent health and spirits. The weather was fine, and the season had opened well. There was more than one visitor in the coffee-room, and business was going on, and the private apartments going off, at a rate of which nobody could complain.

Paul had a grand scheme in his head for

re-commencing his search after Helen, and
the very day after his arrival, took the precaution of dropping a line to Mr. Bloss, to
inquire if he was quite sure that she was
still at large. An answer by return of post,
brought him Mr. Bloss' compliments, and
an assurance that the five hundred pounds
still remained unclaimed.

It began to strike him, however, before
he had been more than a day or two in the
hotel, that although nobody could be more
civil or attentive than were Mr. Maldon and
his wife, there was something in their manner not altogether as cordial as before.
Nothing is more difficult to analyse than
the conduct of our acquaintance, when, for
some undiscoverable reason, we are obliged
to suspect that they like us less than for-
merly. In Paul's case, the change in their
behaviour, although utterly indescribable in

words, was sufficiently marked to occasion him both annoyance and surprise.

His landlord, however, was not a man to keep things to himself, or to expend needless curiosity upon his customers for want of asking questions. So, a few days after Paul's arrival, during a conversation respecting rifle-practice and volunteering in general, he suddenly broke ground.

"Seen Mr. Tobacco to-day, sir?" he inquired mysteriously.

"Seen whom?" retorted Paul, puzzled. "O, I recollect. The dirty little rascal you told me was a spy. Not I! By the way, it's odd enough, but, do you know, the day I left your house last, he got into the train after me—followed me all the way to London Bridge Station—and saw me off to Paris!"

"I know he did," remarked Mr. Maldon gravely, and with an oracular nod.

"Come, come, my good friend, what the
deuce is the matter with you? Tell us
what you mean, and have done with it. Only
don't cock your head, and say ' I knew it,'
like a bully at the Old Bailey."

"Beg your pardon, sir, I'm sure," replied Mr. Maldon, with the air of a man
unwilling to give offence,—" but the trouble
seems to be about those notes, sir ; as you
must surely know."

"Trouble! What trouble? What notes?
My good friend, pray don't equivocate, but
speak your mind at once, if you've got one."

" Well then, sir; as we were saying in
this very parlour—you and me and Mrs.
Maldon together, not so many evenings back
—there were three Thousand Pound notes
lost by Admiral Mortlake of Riverwood over
yonder, in a red leather pocket-book. Well,
those notes were not only advertised, of

course, to be brought to the Bank here, but
two chaps—inspectives, detectors, or whatever one should call them—were sent down
from London, just to rout out, as we understood, all about these bank notes, and make
plain, as it were, why they didn't turn up.
And a precious lot of questions they asked,
to be sure; as much about Miss Helen as
the notes, so I hear—as if she was likely to
have found them, poor young lady. Well,
at last, they went away, leaving word that
it was all most uncommonly odd. ' No need
to come all the way from London to tell us
that,' says we. Well, and when they went
away, they left that little prowling chap
behind them, what for I don't know. Always drinking at the ' Six Bells,' close by
the Bank, he is. Well sir, and when you
went into the Bank t'other morning, and
asked Mr. Crackleton, the Manager, quite

sudden, and as it were sagacious, about these
very notes ; and told him to take the consequences, and all that sort of thing, if he
didn't let out all he knew before you left the
counter, why Mr. Crackleton, very naturally,
I mean for him, took it into his head that
he should like to know a little who you
might be — thinking you wouldn't likely
have asked the question just for the mere
fun of the thing. I'm only telling you, sir,
simply what I hear, you know, and, what
with being churchwarden, and all that, I
naturally do hear a good deal of what goes
on up at St. Mark's. And so, as I couldn't
and shouldn't have thought of giving Mr.
Crackleton any information about you, sir,
even if, in fact, I'd had any to give, and
wouldn't hear him mention the matter twice
over, what does he do but set this chap,
Tobacco, to dodge about here, and track you

all the way right up to London, till he
could lay the regulars on, don't you see?
That's what he was up to. Only you gave
him the slip. That you did! They never
expected you were going foreign, not they,
and didn't find him money enough for that
sort of travel. Besides, he can't talk French,
of course, or anything over the way; not
even if he kept sober on purpose to try. So
you got away, don't you see? I'm told he
cried like a pump, all over the platform,
directly the train started."

"Go on," retorted Paul, severely.

"Well sir—ever since you've been back
here, I've noticed him as it were snuffing
about after you. He ain't a pleasant follower
to have about one, is he? He asked me a
question or two, only last night; and said
it might be worth a ten-pound note to him
yet, to keep his eye on you."

" I don't know what he values his eye at.
Under ten pounds, I hope. Go on."

" Well, that's about all, sir. I'm sure
I've meant no offence. I'm sure it's all
quite right. I've made Mrs. Maldon quite
clear as to that, sir. She's of the same mind
as I am. I *know* it's all right, sir. I'll take
my oath to that, as soon as you like. Pray,
sir, name something that I can have the
pleasure of doing for you."

" If you will have the goodness to let my
bill be made out within ten minutes, I
shall be obliged."

Poor Mr. Maldon! He was absolutely
unconscious of having done wrong. He had
been a little inquisitive to be sure ; and had
told Paul, unasked, what other people had
said of him. And yet he fancied that he
was either very roughly treated, or that
Paul must be a perfect Claude Duval. So
little was he versed in mankind.

Still, it is only justice to Paul, to observe that, great as the provocation may have been, it was aggravated in the sudden overthrow of his grand scheme, which was thenceforth out of the question.   To go gossipping and ferretting about, with Mr. Tobacco at his heels, doing as much for him, would be too ridiculous.   Besides, it could end in nothing less than homicide.   It occurred to him, to be sure, that he might go to the Bank and explain, once for all, who he was, and what little good could come of dogging him. But the obvious retort would be :—" You may be, as you say, Mr. Petersfeld of the Albany, and we are quite willing to believe you respectable : but what made you ask that extraordinary question about the bank notes? What business was it of yours?   You must have had some reason.   Satisfy us, as to that, and we will let you alone and welcome."

And, what answer was it possible for him to give? To tell the truth was out of the question, whilst to invent an excuse, even if such ingenuity could have been justifiable, was altogether beyond his power.

It was a severe blow. Was this to be the end of all his vaunted energy and resolution, of which we heard so much at first starting? Shouldering his knapsack, and informing his conscience-stricken host that, under the circumstances of the case, it was impossible that he should prolong his sojourn at St. Mark's Bay, he marched straight for the railway station. What he meant to do —whether to return to town at once, and send for the tailor and Linda to divide him between them, or how otherwise to dispose of himself, he had not made up his mind. In short, he not only didn't know where he was going, but, what is more remarkable, it is quite certain that the fact never will be known.

For, on his way up the long straggling street already described, and when just opposite the " Six Bells," there came a loud cheery shout from a small, stout man, who had just mounted a copper-coloured pony before the door.

" Hoy! I say, sir, how d'ye do—how d'ye do ?"

" Well, much as usual, thank ye !" replied Paul, taking the friendly inquiry for market chaff; " Remember me kindly when you get home !"

" No, but, hoy! hang it! Stop, won't you, Mr. —— I forget your name ?"

" Why, *you*, Mr. Bunnytail !"

Paul was one of those lucky people who never seem to confuse names or faces, and have the former always handy for use.

" Thank'ye sir, I'm sure, for recollecting
me. It was at Master Buttermere's we met
last, wasn't it? Something like a blow out,
that was! Will you come across and see
us, sir, now that you're close by? Make
my good lady as happy as a Princess Royal,
that would. You'll do it, won't you?"

Mr. Bunnytail called his fat wife his good
lady, and revered her as a bloated aristocrat,
in consequence of her connection with the
Buttermeres. To be redolent of Harley
Street, was rank and precedence at Bunnytail Bottom.

There was no reason in the world why
Paul should not accept the good-natured
invitation. His time was his own, and
Bunnytail Bottom as good a base of operations as St. Mark's-on-the-Sea. Better, in
fact. Indeed, this meeting seemed a piece
of unusual good luck.

"Do you really mean, Mr. Bunnytail, that you would offer me a night's lodging? I was just on my way to catch the next train for London; at least, that would have been the end of it, for I've had about enough of St. Mark's. But I'll leave London alone for to-day, and pay you and Mrs. Bunnytail a visit with the greatest possible pleasure."

"Come, that's kind now! Lodging for the night, indeed!" exclaimed the farmer, who absorbed ideas gradually, and to whom a moderately long sentence was worse travelling than a ploughed field. "Lodging for the night? that's good! That would be a joke, indeed, wouldn't it? Say three weeks, Master Petersfeld—say a month. The longer the better. That's to say if you should be spared so long; as it's hardly reasonable to hope you will."

"Spared so long!" echoed Petersfeld. "I

hope I'm not on my last legs yet! Not got
anything infectious down your way, I hope.
No cholera?"

"Lord love you, no! 'Twasn't that sort
of sparing I meant. But if somebody that
I mustn't name, I suppose—leastways, only
as Venus, as my good lady would say—
could only spare you, I'll be bound we won't
quarrel about anything till you come to
speak about starting. My good lady, down
yonder, has talked of nothing but you, for the
last two days and more; nothing whatever."

"Talked of me! Very kind of her, I'm
sure. Why she should have taken the
trouble to recollect my name at all, is more
than I can imagine."

"Eh!" exclaimed the farmer, with a tremendous wink. "Quite fair, sir, quite fair;
ha, ha, ha! But now let's see. Out with
the filly directly, Joe, and clap the new

saddle on. Dust her down, Joe, and look alive. And then, Joe, you step over to the Bottom with this gent's knapsack. That's about the time of day, sir! Won't my good lady be proud and happy," continued he, looking at Petersfeld with the sort of honest pride which comes over anglers when they regard a twenty-four pound salmon fairly landed on the grass.

Just at that moment, the postman passed, and handed my letter to Petersfeld. "For you, I think, sir? It's directed to the St. Mark's Bay Hotel. I believe you were staying there."

" Quite right, thank you. O, from Worsley, I see. Wonder what the old boy's found to write about!" And Paul thrust the note, unopened, into his breast-pocket, for he was extremely curious to know what Mr. Bunny-tail meant.

"Aye, she's talked of you, off and on," resumed the farmer, as they jogged along down a by-street, ever since that day she met you at the Zoological Gardens, you recollect, and you sent her home half-seas over with cherry bounce. Ever since that famous dinner at Master Buttermere's, when we spoke, I remember, about that handsome young woman as had run away, and was going to be rewarded if anybody could find her. I'm not much of a reader, myself, and I never saw the story in print. Not found yet, sir, I suppose, is she?"

"Not that I'm aware of. By the way, Mr. Bunnytail, you told me, if I was lucky enough to find her myself, to bring her to Bunnytail Bottom."

"So I did, sure enough, and so I do. What I mean, I say, Mr. Petersfeld, and what I say, I mean. And welcome you are to do it any day. Ah, yes : now I recollect the whole story. She ran away because she didn't want to stay at home—wasn't that it? And they offered a reward for her per-secution. More shame for them, I say. Oh, yes. You bring her to Bunnytail Bot-tom, and let's see if they'll persecute her there. Not while I've a cart-whip and a horse-pond on the premises. She'll be quite company for you, Mr. Petersfeld, won't she? O, no! Bless me—I forgot. That would never do now, would it?"

"Really, Mr. Bunnytail, you are deter-mined to puzzle me. Come, *that's* no use ! You might wink your eye out without making me any the wiser. And, if you're bent upon poking me off my horse with that big whip of yours—why, do it at once, and get it over."

"Eh?" chuckled the farmer, who was

manifestly labouring under that tremendous
amount of internal pressure characteristic of
pastoral badinage, "Quite fair, sir, quite
fair! ha, ha, ha!"

As there is nothing to which even the
most good-natured people, who have not
been brought up to it, feel a more wholesome
aversion than waggery of this description,
Paul changed the subject as soon as possible,
and their talk ran upon bullocks and barley,
all the way to Bunnytail Bottom.

CHAPTER III.

I AM not going to put your patience to the
test by any laboured description of the agri-
cultural retreat, which for little less than
a century, had been the modest castle of
Clan Bunnytail. I will only say that the
first *coup d'œil* presented a large, comfortable, rambling farmhouse of the olden style.
Around and behind rose outbuildings, barns,
granaries, stables, cow-sheds, and piggywig-
geries, upon the most extensive scale; and a
grand rookery, too, from which the birds
hoorayed in airy chorus, as if celebrating
the new arrival.

This was all that Petersfeld was able to

take in at the moment, for he was immediately ushered into the parlour. Much as
Mr. Bunnytail would have liked to have
had the drawing-room arrayed for reception,
and his good lady adorned to match, it was
clearly out of the question. It would never
have done to keep Petersfeld waiting; whilst
to postpone the triumph of presenting him,
was simply impossible.

Accordingly, with buoyant alacrity, Mr.
Bunnytail danced into the room, hustling
Paul before him as if he had been caught
stealing eggs. "Mr. Petersfeld, Madam!
Madam, Mr. Petersfeld!" he exclaimed, with
eager voice and sparkling eyes; and then,
tucking his riding-whip under his coat-tail,
straightened himself up into an attitude of
profound, yet respectful curiosity, waiting
to see how the 'nobs' would behave.

Mrs. Bunnytail looked, strange to say,

several layers larger in her own house, than
she had appeared at the Buttermere dinner.
Perhaps the smallness of the parlour caused
an apparent difference. Perhaps the fact
that instead of being tightly girthed in, and
properly saddled and bridled, she was
dressed in the loosest possible costume, out
of which nevertheless she was, in the most
unmistakable manner, bursting at every
seam. Perhaps she was still growing. She
reminded Paul, indeed, of the lobster at the
Zoological Gardens, when in the act of
splitting up his old shell, preparatory to
starting a new suit.

The three impish children sat at play on
the carpet, diverting themselves with sheeps'
knuckle bones. There is a base mediæval
game, which it appears can be played with
no nicer materials. I fancy I remember it
at school, under the name of 'dibs.'

Whatever Mrs. Bunnytail may have been doing, when Paul entered the room, she seemed heartily ashamed of detection; and tumbled a large basket hastily into the corner before she could collect herself sufficiently to recognise her visitor.

" Mr.—Petersfeld—?" she exclaimed, at last, as she rose amazed from her sofa with the air of a person who gradually becomes aware of an apparition. " Mr. Petersfeld ? Is it possible ? Oh, how truly kind to come all the way from London, and bring us the good news yourself !"

And, before Paul had leisure even to imagine a reply, the good lady, sailing across the floor, had clasped him to her bosom, and imprinted upon his expostulating lips half a dozen of such smacking kisses as made the room ring again.

" And all in such a moment, too !" continued the lady. "O, I was happy to get Carlo's letter! Not but that I knew well enough what was in the wind; only it seemed almost too good to be true. Jump up, you little rogues, and kiss your new cousin; and thank him for coming here to-day."

"Mrs. Bunnytail!" exclaimed Paul, as soon as he could find breath to speak, "What is the meaning of all this? You must be dreaming!"

A dreadful suspicion—and then a certainty had flashed upon his mind almost at the same moment; and a dream of the night, long since forgotten, was remembered with intolerable accuracy.

"Dreaming indeed! Well done you, Paul. Why, when you're Linda's husband, and that's as good as done, shan't I be your aunt, and Bunnytail there, your uncle? and won't these precious pets be all your own cousins? O, what a blessed thing relationship is—isn't it, Paul, my dear?"

"Seems about the right way to take it, don't it, nephey?" struck in Mr. Bunnytail, respectfully; observing the blank look of utter and indignant astonishment with which this rapid sketch of a new position was accepted.

"But I have no sort of intention of marrying Miss Linda Buttermere, or anybody else," retorted Paul. "The whole thing's a delusion ; and I wish to Heaven you'd let it alone !"

"Not marry my niece !" screamed Mrs. Bunnytail. "What are you going to do to her then, Paul? What have I got ears to hear, for—and eyes to read writing, for —and Carlo's letter in my pocket, for, if you ain't going to marry her. O, Petersfeld, you astonish me now, indeed."

"Hoity, toity !" chimed in her husband ;

not so much for the value of the remark, as from fear of being twitted with 'want of spirit,' if he said nothing at all.

"You will rue the day, and rue the hour, when you did this, you know," continued the lady, portentously.

"Damages, nephey," commented the farmer, with a grave roll of his head.

"Yes you will indeed, Paul. This night shall my sister Carlo learn what it is most meet that she should know. But, Paul—if I may still call you Paul—you're not in earnest, are you, really? You're only playing off your fun upon us, as I do hope and believe. Oh, Paul, if you was to turn out a scoundrel, it would break the whole set of hearts in our family."

"Mine, anyhow," came from Mr. Bunnytail, with a profound sniff.

What to do with our nerves when we

don't want them, is one of the grandest
secrets in the world. How to keep cool
under red-hot pressure, and leisurely 'take
occasion by the hand' instead of being run
away with by ourselves, is a problem very
deep. Paul had gone through his course at
Hythe, and perhaps had picked it up there.
At any rate, with all his tendency to impulsive and immediate action, he could sometimes be cool where coolness was indispensable, and think in a critical moment. Just
then, he certainly had need of all his savoir
faire. To have stubbornly withstood this
overwhelming woman and her husband
would have ended in his being turned out
of the house. Not that this would have
been any such irreparable calamity; but
goodness only knew what was in store for him
in Harley Street, or how far Mrs. Bunnytail might contrive to complicate matters.

"If you would only allow me one moment to explain, Mrs. Bunnytail," he said, "I feel confident that we should understand each other. You will listen to me, will you not?"

"O, if you want to explain," remarked Mrs. Bunnytail, bridling loftily, "go on, Mr. Petersfeld, as long as you please."

To a certain order of minds, the idea of an explanation is associated with a contrite attitude, and a miserable hope of being forgiven.

"As long as you please, nephey," repeated Mr. Bunnytail. "You shall speak the truth, and the whole truth, and nothing but the truth, mind; because, so help you, that's the law. Will you take a nip of something, nephey, before you confess? Beer—brandy —or gooseberry wine? Only put a name to it, nephey. It may be a help, don't you see?"

"Thank you," replied Petersfeld, feeling very much as if he were in the custody of a couple of orang-outangs, at their private residence in Java, "I think I can get through it without assistance. Of course, Mrs. Bunnytail, your sister, Mrs. Buttermere, is in the habit of giving you the very earliest information upon all points of family interest?"

"That she is, Peter—I mean Paul," replied the lady. "You may depend upon that. For I say to her always, Carlo, say I,—Do you tell me all that is right and proper I should know, and behave true and handsome to me, as I to you, and then all's fair and square between us. But don't you think to play hide-and-seek with me, because I don't stand that at any price ; and if I haven't news from you, to tell the Shankers, and the Greens, and the Beestleys, and the

Swabstalls, and the rest of my neighbours,
why I'll invent for my credit sake.   I ain't
going to have it whispered about that my
sister in Harley Street looks down upon me
from the top windows of her haughty man-
sion, and that I don't know more of what
goes on inside than the scullion in her
kitchen."

" My good lady has the soul of a noble-
woman, and well she may," remarked Mr.
Bunnytail, admiringly.

" To be sure.   But do you know, Mrs.
Bunnytail, that what you have just told me,
seems to afford a simple explanation of the
whole matter."

" Not to me," interrupted the lady sharply.
" Not one bit of good your explaining, if I
ain't made happy and satisfied."

" Of course not.   But I am sure you must
have observed that engagements of this kind,

always supposing them to exist at all, invariably occupy some considerable time among the higher circles—"

"Oh, yes! That may be. But they always come to the same thing in the end."

"Not always, Mrs. Bunnytail, as your experience of society will remind you. Now, my dear madam," continued Petersfeld, "the fact, I am confident, is this,—Your sister, Mrs. Buttermere, in her anxiety to afford you the earliest possible information upon an interesting subject, has been slightly premature. She has told you what she no doubt believed was, or would turn out to be, the truth ; but before it was at all wise to mention it even among relations. You would not have done so by her, had the case been reversed. Your better judgment would have induced you to withhold all information upon so delicate a subject—even to a sister

—until there could be no longer the possibility of mistake."

" Mistake, indeed!" cried Mrs. Bunnytail,
who was rapidly getting out of her depth.
" Why, as I said just now, what had I got
eyes to see for, and ears to hear for, in
Harley Street, let alone the Zoological Gardens, which was a sight in itself?   Ah, you
won't get out of that, Paul, my man, in a
hurry!   And what have I got Carlo's letter
in my pocket for at this very moment?
What's the meaning of this?" continued
she, producing the document referred to from
some extraordinary marsupial cavity—" How
about half-a-dozen chemises trimmed with
Valenciennes lace, and as many with worked
edges?   How about six white petticoats, all
with rich flouncing, and coloured skirts em-
broidered and braided?   How about silk
stockings and pocket-handkerchiefs, and all

the rest of it?   What's Linda to be trussed
for if she ain't going to be married? Answer
me that, Paul!"

Petersfeld grew desperate.   The foolish
mamma had evidently made up her mind
that he was safely hooked; and had not
only imparted the fact to her sister, but—
for fear of being suspected of suppressing a
material fact—had regaled her with the description of a possible trousseau, for the
edification of her country friends.

"I tell you what, Mrs. Bunnytail," he
exclaimed, without further care or caution,
"this is going a little too far! Linda and
I have only met twice in our lives, and all
the rest is mistake and delusion. If you
don't choose to believe me, all I can say is
that this moment I leave your house. I'll
go up in a balloon, or down a mine, or right
away to the end of Egypt, and never come

back till I hear Linda's married and done for! You're enough to drive a man mad among you. Yes—you may look as you like, but I'll stand no more of this idiotic non-sense; and so good-bye to you both."

"Good-bye, indeed! Not if B. does his duty. B., do it like a man! Don't let him go. Stand up for your own niece. Fight for her, B. !"

Fighting for anybody was entirely out of Mr. Bunnytails' line; but standing as he did in ghostly and bodily fear of his wife, especially when invoked as a simple con-sonant, he prepared for the worst. Hoping something, perhaps, from a little experi-mental demonstration, he began by backing against his parlour door, and saying ' Wo— ho !' like a carter.

"Come, come, my good friends, all this is foolish. You don't think you are going to

arrest me, I suppose. Why not part without quarrelling, if we can? Mr. Bunnytail,
you appear to be trying to sit down, which
is impossible upon a perpendicular surface.
Hadn't you better come back to your
chair?"

"B! Why don't you seize him, before he
escapes?" cried the good lady, at the top of
her voice.

"Madam, because I'm not so sure he'd let
me loose again," replied her husband, brush-
ing the wall behind him in all directions,
with his eyes fixed on Petersfeld, like a
comet with tail turned away from the sun.
"My nephey's blood's up. I can see that.
Now, look here, you two! Can't we see a cool
and kindly way out of all this? So long as
nephey likes to stay with us here, and the
longer the better say we both, why not promise to say nothing to nobody? Why

should we? So long as he's safe to hand, where's the good of driving on matters? They'll come all right in the end, I'll be bound. He's not up to the mark at present, madam, our nephey ain't. That's clear as the day. Look at him. Lean as a tree, with no red about him anyhow. Let me feed him up here for a fortnight, and he'll take off his hat to himself in a glass, that he will! He's pining now: nothing else. Won't be fit for trussing for ever so long. Come, madam, what do you say?"

After considerable discussion, Mrs. Bunnytail was induced to promise that, so long as Paul chose to consider himself as one of the family at Bunnytail Bottom, and made no attempt to elope without warning, she would refrain from denouncing him to her sister in Harley Street.

Not that she gave her consent without

misgivings of the most complicated description, which were all volubly reviewed for Paul's benefit. But her husband, who, to do him justice, was animated by all good feeling, and actuated by considerable good sense, ultimately carried his point.

As for Paul, he certainly was to be pitied. The humiliation of being pounced upon by a farmer's wife, and finding himself after capture, a sort of prisoner on parole, was a horrible absurdity. But what was he to do? Was he to allow himself to be driven out of the house, as he had been out of the St. Mark's Bay Hotel, by his own oversensitiveness, and roam the country like a wandering Jew? Was he to permit this disastrous woman to write what she liked of him to the Buttermeres, and not only keep the dreadful question alive, but perhaps render any satisfactory solution impossible?

Was he to give up his pursuit altogether, and return to Stone Buildings a beaten man, with his character for energy disposed of altogether, in exchange for the consequences of a painful and deplorable blunder?

He resolved to sacrifice everything for a little breathing time, and with very bad grace—it must be confessed—re-accepted the farmer's hospitality, and consented to make himself at home at Bunnytail Bottom.

The preliminaries of peace thus settled, were ratified by the high contracting parties over a tea of tremendous proportions. Story-tellers are fond of making ill-natured fun of these rustic hospitalities, and describing the amount of home-made bread, reeking toast, and pig in all its phases, forced upon the distended and perspiring guest. However, I can safely say that all

descriptions which I ever read, fall short of
a reality in which I was myself an actor.
Probably I have got hold of the wrong word.
I don't imagine that the Dean of Canter-
bury would allow a man to be an actor
(active) who only sat impatiently still to be
stuffed (passive). But I declare that I left
the table with some thoughts of having
myself stamped ' proof,' like a gun-barrel,
since, after that, whatever may happen to
me, I am certain never to burst.

Next morning Petersfeld was called out
of bed at cock-crow, to behold the milk-
ing, and the whole forenoon was devoted to
a grand inspection of the farm and its
belongings. Bunnytail was delighted with
his visitor, and made no secret of his contempt for the policy which had cut up the
making of a first-rate farmer, to manufac-
ture nothing better than a limb of the law.

Solomon the bull was first visited, praised and patted, and his various points of ex-cellence, and noble pedigree, enlarged upon with unsparing eloquence. And once set going, Bunnytail took care that Paul should know no rest, until he was almost as well acquainted with the stock and premises as he was himself. Like Farmer Philip in the idyll, taking our young friend remorse-lessly in tow, .

> " He led him through the short sweet-smelling lanes
> Of his wheat suburb, babbling as he went.
> He praised his land, his horses, his machines ;
> He praised his ploughs, his cows, his hogs, his dogs ;
> He praised his hens, his geese, his guinea-hens ;
> His pigeons, who, in session on their roofs,
> Approved him, bowing at their own deserts.
> Then from the plaintive mother's teat he took
> Her blind and shuddering puppies, naming each ;"

And so on, until another gluttonous bell announced the hour of noon, and that the board was again covered, for more serious work than ever.

Dinner over, Petersfeld was pleased to find his host and hostess retire to their respective arm-chairs, and begin to snore, like a couple of old-fashioned giants.

Availing himself of the welcome opportunity he lost no time in turning out for a quiet stroll. "O, solitude, where are thy charms?" may have been the song of Alexander Selkirk. To any person undergoing a course of penal education upon the 'separate system,' the absolute immunity from interruption, and the liberty of pursuing, in consequence, any desirable train of thought to its utmost limit, may savour of what gourmands deprecate as *toujours perdrix*. But as clothes to the cold, food to the famishing, sleep to the weary, and balm to broken heads, so is perfect loneliness to one who has been bored to extinction, and escaped as by a miracle. We seem to drift idly on, through sheets of delicious calm, and the very sensation of existence becomes, in itself, enjoyable.

But Petersfeld had a great deal to think about. Now or never, was the time to put into execution the grand scheme of which we have already heard. What this scheme was, I need hardly be at the trouble of telling you, for reasons which you will discover for yourself, before you have read five pages further. I will only say that it was based upon the fact that, by his recent journey to Paris, he had ascertained, beyond all possibility of doubt, that Helen had *not* left home with her friends, and that consequently he felt himself released from all obligation to conduct his enquiries with the care and reticence which he had scrupu-

lously observed whilst that question remained open. He knew, now, that something was wrong somewhere, and that people
had been deliberately deceived. He there-
fore considered himself at liberty to act
upon his own discretion, and cut, if he
could, the knot which appeared so difficult
to untie, without further ceremony.

Just at that moment, while rummaging
for his cigar-case, he pulled out my still
unopened letter. Its contents horrified
him. Matters had been black enough before, but he had always trusted that the
misconception, as between himself and Linda,
was one which would right itself easily
enough, and that he might at least count
upon Buttermere's practical good sense to
view the matter in its proper light, should
it ever become sufficiently serious to call for
his attention. But to find that the latter had

already taken it up in such uncompromising
earnest, was a frightful fact, and seemed for
the moment to paralyse his energies altogether.   So this was the result of that fatal
advertisement !

Angry, irresolute, and in utter despair, he
wandered for hours about the country, won-
dering what was the best thing to be done.
To rush off instantly to London, and ask
my own advice, was his first impulse.   To
be sure, Mrs. Bunnytail would consider him
a deserter, and send hue and cry after him
by the evening post.   But that was of little
consequence, as matters stood.   It might be
more gracious, after all, to go back for his
knapsack, and wish his late entertainers a
proper good-bye.   He had still plenty of
time.   It was but little after three o'clock,
and it might be better not to arrive in
London before dark.

His meditations were interrupted, or rather his attention distracted, by finding that he had quite inadvertently arrived at the boundary of the Riverwood estate. He had approached it, in fact, from a direction contrary to that which he had previously taken, and his proximity was altogether a surprise. A low stone wall was all that separated him from the pleasure-grounds, and within little more than a hundred yards from the road, he could distinguish the tiny weathercock which surmounted Helen's summer-house, veering and twinkling in the sun.

Nothing could have been more disconcerting at the moment. "It is well," he growled, "that I should own myself a fool and an impostor, upon this particular spot. I have thrown away both time and money in a pursuit which none but a lunatic would have undertaken, and I am justly punished by finding myself in a scrape of which goodness only knows the end. No matter! I am awake at last. I will clear my mind of the whole of this egregious business whilst I can. In that arbour I will stand and swear the most solemn oath I can think of, to abandon this accursed chase for ever, and try to be wiser through time to come. Energy, indeed! I hate the word. Mine has been the energy of Milo—if the comparison isn't too preposterously in his favour. Let me only find my hands loose again, and Worsley may thrash me like a donkey, before I give another kick without reason. As to this Miss Fleetlands," continued he, striding leisurely over the fence, "from this moment I wash my hands of her rights and wrongs. I only wish I had never heard of her. Positively, if I found her at this moment, sewn up in a sack, and labelled 'Constantinople,' I wouldn't interfere—unless I saw them going to hang her upside down. So now, then!"

As Paul reached the summer-house, the door was quietly unlocked, and a young lady descended the steps.

She was dressed in brown silk, with a purple cloth jacket; and her white straw hat, trimmed with black velvet, was ornamented with a grey grebe feather.

Paul staggered and started back.

He knew at once that it was Helen.

A sudden thrill shot through every fibre. A sensation, such as few experience more than once in a lifetime, held him planted where he stood.

As for Helen, she sprang forward, with a half-uttered exclamation of delight' and then, violently trembling, drew back, cold and pale.

In the bewilderment of sudden meeting, and amid the shadow of the yews, she had mistaken Paul for Ferdinand.

CHAPTER IV.

AND how came Helen there?

Fortunately for you, if you are disposed to put the question, it is one which in due course of story-telling must at once receive a solution.

We left her hurrying from her Guardian's room, towards that precious depository in the garden, whither all materials for, as she hoped, complete and impenetrable disguise had already been so carefully transported. Once there, the work of disfigurement was rapid enough. Her usual dress was thrown off in a moment, and as quickly locked up in a cupboard. And the slops, which came out in exchange, not only made her look seriously old at once, but, having been padded after the light of nature, gave her a buxom aspect in the way of waist and shoulders, which at once rendered identification impossible.

A touch or so of colour, rubbed on at random, produced a result which was quite reassuring, as examined in her pocket-mirror. To attach a small bit of black sticking-plaister to one of her front teeth was the next process ; but the result was so hideously successful that feminine philosophy gave way, and the experiment was abandoned. However, when her bonnet was at last tied tight under chin—her shawl adjusted house-maid fashion—her basket on her arm, and a pair of fat worsted gloves, which were a feature in themselves, assumed, to make all complete, she would have liked nothing better than to drop a curtsey to the Admiral himself.

Whatever may have been her sensations as she stepped lightly over the stile which bounded the Riverwood property, and marched for the first time in her life an independent traveller upon the Queen's highway, she started with unwavering pluck and resolution. It was too late to look back; and there was not much use in looking forward, for that matter. Events would have to shape themselves; and so she trudged straight to the Bunnytail Station, certain admonitory lines ringing warning as she walked.

> " 'Tis said that the Lion will turn and flee
> From a maid in the pride of her purity,
> But, anyhow, if she's a wise little thing,
> She'll steer quite clear of the Beastly King!"

Luckily for her, the Lion happened not

to be abroad that evening, and she arrived within view of the station without the necessity of exchanging a word with any one.

"Come along, Jess!" exclaimed a young woman, in a weary tone, who was walking in the same direction, upon the opposite side of the road. "You keep up with me, or you'll be left behind."

"Can't, mother," replied Jess, with a shrill sob. "It's the bundle won't come—not me!"

"Well, you must make it. I've got the. child to carry, and ever so much besides. You'll hear the train-bell ring next; and then we shall be lost, and no mistake."

"Ain't much further, mother, is it?"

"No. Not a step, scarcely. Can't you see those lights yonder?"

"Can't see nothing over the bundle," gasped the unfortunate mite, hugging the unwieldy affair to her bosom, as if it had been the dearest friend she had in the world.

"Poor little thing," exclaimed Helen, good-naturedly crossing the road. "You carry my bag for me, and I'll carry the bundle. That will be fair enough, won't it?"

"Yes, thanky!" gasped Jess, delighted. "I'll carry the bag for you, and no mistake."

"Don't do no such thing, ma'am," interposed the mother. "It's not for the like of you to be carrying our baggage. We'll do well enough, and thank you all the same. It's not far to go, now."

"Nonsense!" said Helen. "Who do you take me for, I wonder. Poor people must help one another."

"Well, it's very kind of you, I'm sure, ma'am; but I'm afraid you'll find the bundle over-heavy."

"What makes you call me ma'am?" de-

manded Helen, impatiently. "Can't you
see that I'm not a lady? You are going by
train, I suppose. So am I." It was rather
too bad to be detected by the first tramp
she met.

Perhaps had her new acquaintance been
better up in poetry than she probably was,
she might have retorted, with the Seneschal
of Artornish :—

> "Worship and birth to me are known
>   By look—by bearing, and by tone :
>   Not by furred robe, or broidered zone."

But, having no such resource at command,
she merely murmured—" No offence, miss,
and thank you kindly. Jess, little maid,
mind and carry careful. Don't you drop
the bag whatever you do. Hush, baby
darling, we're almost home now."

"And we'll see daddy again there, won't
we, mother?" cried Jess, skipping along with

the bag. "You know you said we should see him again, didn't you ?"

There was no answer to this question. The baby was only rolled round and smothered with kisses. It was not until they reached the bridge over the line, that a quiet husky voice said — "Yes, we are going by the train. We have a long way to travel."

"So have I," observed Helen, gently. "How far do you go to-night?"

"All the way to Izzleworth town."

"Just where I'm going myself."

"Is it indeed!" exclaimed the young woman. "But I dare say you'll travel— not with us. You go third-class too, though, perhaps," she added, nervously ; trusting that in this daring attempt to get right, she was not blundering beyond all possibility of forgiveness.

"Third-class! yes, I'm going third-class, like you," replied Helen, clutching eagerly at anything like companionship. "I've no money to throw away, I assure you. Do you know what the fare comes to?"

"Twelve shillings, ma'am, the full-sized ticket, and six shillings for Jess. Eighteen shillings, with nothing in the world to show for it at the other end. It's like flinging money all about in the dirt, isn't it? It's all the same to them, I should say, whether I get in or not. If I don't, where's their eighteen shillings? If I do, what odds does it make to the train? If I'd got another eighteen shillings, I shouldn't mind so much. But I haven't."

"Well, take a ticket for me," said Helen, producing her money. "I'll mind Jess and the traps. Say you want another ticket for your sister, then they'll be sure to put us all together, and it's lonely travelling without some one to talk to."

Unhesitatingly committing herself to this very shallow piece of strategy, the woman soon returned with the tickets; and, almost at the same moment, a pair of calm expanding eyes, devouring the dusk, appeared in the distance. Helen held Jess tight by the hand, so that neither could run away. Then the bell rang; the train pulled up with a crash and a grind, looking weird and large as train never looked before, with lamps burning, and people smoking. "Any one for Bunnytail? Third-class, behind! Now then, young woman, look alive!" And the guard hustled Helen and her companions into a third-class compartment, and blew his whistle, before he shut the door with a bang.

"That's a nice steady man, and I should like to give him a shilling," thought Helen.

"He can trust his own eyes. People like that give no trouble."

I may as well notice here, by way of parenthesis, that it was to this fortunate encounter upon the road, that Helen was indebted for the chief element of mystery which surrounded her disappearance—perhaps for making a successful business of it at all.

The station-master at Bunnytail, in answer to close and persistent interrogatories, was so confident that nobody had left his station by that particular train, which happened to be the latest of the day, except two females with babies and bundles, who took third-class tickets, that the detectives gave up the rail theory altogether. Oddly enough, at the St. Marks Station, they fancied that they had got hold of a clue, which they followed with profound sagacity as far as St.

Bees, where they overhauled the wrong lady, and re-appeared in disgrace.

The journey passed quietly enough. There were several people in the compartment, and the only thing which struck Helen as remarkable, was a sort of honest spontaneous friendliness which is not cultivated in coupés and first-class carriages. Nobody seemed to feel that a remark needed an apology, or that the commonest act of civility might be construed as an affront. On the contrary, an old lady, who at once addressed the mother as 'my dear,' overflowed with valuable advice as to the nurture and admonition of the baby; while a working man, after offering Jess tobacco by way of introduction, took her upon his lap and conjured lollipops out of his trousers' pocket. Indeed, he seemed to have quite a quantity of these delicacies binned away somewhere about him, for he gave them away right and left, and one which he presented to Helen was speckled all over with sawdust, and tasted of timber.

The story which the poor woman had to tell, and which it seemed to be a relief to her to tell again and again, was sad, not strange. Her husband, a carpenter at St. Marks, had died suddenly a few weeks before. In an instant the blight and the shadow of death fell upon all that he had left behind. Her home was broken up, her furniture sold, and that 'daily bread,' for which, I am afraid, too many of us pray like parrots every morning, with about as much earnestness as if asking that the sun may continue to shine, and the earth to revolve as usual, was no longer forthcoming for her children's meals. In despair, she was making her way to her late husband's father in Izzleworth—not hoping much, poor soul; for 'the more the merrier,' is a welcome only heard in first-class company. And three new mouths to be fed, fresh from a third-class van, could only, as she was aware, come down like a calamity upon a household in which daily bread had not only to be prayed for, but watched and worked for in good earnest.

It was just as well for Helen that she caught this glimpse of real trouble to compare with her own dissatisfaction. Rarely in early life do we make acquaintance with pain, mental or bodily. And when the truth breaks upon us like a surprise, and we learn the conditions under which we actually live, we are ashamed of the fuss which we used to make in our ignorance, and understand that we have still an education to complete.

"I suppose you'll go to your clergyman

when you get settled, shan't you? said
Helen. What's his name? How old is
he? Perhaps he'll give you a lift."

" Doctor Orchard was our clergyman,
ma'am, when I left Izzleworth—but that's six
years ago. I hope he's not dead too. He
was a nice kind old gentleman as ever lived."

" I think clergymen ought always to be
old. I've no patience with young ones.
They are always conceited, and a great
deal too fond of their own opinion."

" Well, we must all have a beginning,
ma'am, mustn't we ? I'm sure I heard Dr.
Orchard's curate preach a wonderful sermon
once about Daniel in the lion's den. You
should have heard him, ma'am, when he
come to the lions !"

" Very likely. I hope he did you good.
Curates are all very well in their way ; but
as to making a beginning, the worst of

it is that they make it at our expense. However," continued Helen, much relieved by certain information which she had just obtained, "that's a matter which is no business of mine. Poor little Jess! you look as if you had had quite enough of the train. How old is she?"

"Five, ma'am. That is, she will be five next Monday as ever is. Poor thing! we used to keep her birthday."

"I wish you would give her this from me on Monday, will you? I've rolled it up in this piece of paper. Don't open it till then. It's only a trifle, and you can spend it for her."

"Surely, ma'am; and thank you kindly."

It was three sovereigns, which Helen, in generous disregard of the value of money, had privately extracted from her purse, and folded in a neat little packet.

"Do you know, ma'am, I think this must be Izzleworth. That's the factory, where all those lights are. Yes, I should know the place anywhere."

It is not likely that she will ever recognise it anywhere else. But it is a strange sensation, that of hurrying into a new town for the first time by lamp-light. Nothing seems absolutely real. The shadowy buildings—the changing streets, the vague window-lights, the smouldering fires and outlying lantern-pickets on the line side, as the train pulls up, whirl past like pictures in a dream, from which we suddenly recover ourselves bright awake in time for the too practical rush and tussle upon the platform.

As Helen had no luggage to look after, she lost no time in walking courageously into the street. It had always been her

project to apply in the first instance to the
clergyman of the place at which she might
happen to arrive, with a story which, when
it came to be subsequently sifted, she hoped
would be considered as a natural and excus-
able fib. A clergyman, as she innocently
supposed, would hardly dismiss a friendless
young woman into the streets the last thing
at night. It would be almost his duty to
see that she was decently taken care of;
and, if so, something might turn up in the
morning. Moreover, should she find his
ecclesiastical hospitality unsatisfactory, what
could be easier than to slip off a hundred
miles or so without notice, and try the same
experiment elsewhere. This seemed quite
a promising programme, combining all the
amusement of travelling with the advan-
tages of orthodox society. And, so long as
her funds lasted, there seemed no reason

against its being continued until her friends at Riverwood had received a lesson which they would never forget. It was delightful to think of the consternation which must have already begun at the Lawn; but a certain nervous wish to find a roof over her head left her no time to make the most of the reflection.

Asking her way at the first baker's, she paced rapidly along the street, for the shops were being closed, and there was no time to be lost. The red leather note-case began to be a dreadful weight upon her mind. She was heartily vexed with herself for having been wilful enough to take it, for not only did it seem certain that it would either crawl out of her pocket upon its own hook or lead to her being robbed and murdered at the first dark corner, but she had a vague impression that people were sometimes stopped and questioned by constables when found abroad at irregular hours, and searched in case they failed to give a fluent account of themselves. And since it was morally impossible that any piece of autobiology which she could offer at short notice would be considered satisfactory in the presence of these overwhelming documents, there was nothing for it but to hope very heartily that she might be left alone.

Fortunately such was the case. She only fell in with one policeman, to whom she appealed at once, by way of throwing him off his guard. And when the youth pointed carelessly with his thumb, and replied, " Orchard's ? Two doors down there—left hand side," she experienced an indescribable sensation of relief.

Izzleworth Vicarage, as seen in the dusk, was a large, roomy, red-brick building, stand-

ing well back from the road, and protected
in that direction by a broad belt of shrubbery. There was a handsome glass porch
before the door, with a large bell-pull, which
produced an unexpectedly loud noise in
answer to Helen's modest appeal.

A dreadful contingency at once flashed
upon her mind. It might be opened by a
footman! That was a casualty upon which
she had never counted. To stand confronted
with a footman in her absurd disguise; to
be obliged to bandy question and answer,
and to be made the butt of his hideous plea-
santries, would be no common scrape. But
she was in for it now, whatever might
happen, since to retreat was out of the
question.

To her great joy the door was opened by
a florid old lady with a flat candlestick. All
that could be seen at the first glimpse was

a handsome cap, a little nose, a complexion
which reminded you of apples not gathered
yesterday, and a pair of twinkling eyes of
the quick inquisitive order, which at once
began playing upon Helen from head to
foot.

"Well. Now then. Who's this?"

"Is this Doctor Orchard's, ma'am?"

"Why, you've rung the bell. What made
you ring it for, if you didn't know that?
Yes, it is Doctor Orchard's. Now then.
What is it?"

"I should like to see Doctor Orchard, if
you please."

"If I please! Suppose he's not at
home."

Helen's heart sunk within her, if that
solution of a deplorable sensation be ana-
tomically admissible.

"I am very anxious indeed to see him. I

am in this town by mistake, and have nowhere to turn. I only wish to ask if he
could put me in the way of obtaining shelter
for the night. I don't want money, or anything of that sort."

"And how comes it that you are in this
town by mistake, and have nowhere to turn?"
demanded the janitrix, allowing Helen to
enter the hall, but surveying her by such
close candle-light, that it was just as well
she had no whiskers to singe. "What shall
I tell the Doctor? He's busy you see, now,
and don't like being disturbed. Only just
look at the clock. You couldn't possibly, I
suppose, walk back to the station, and take
the train for where you was going, and where
you ought, of course, to be by rights before
this; and then we should have no bother
here, don't you see? They're civil people
at the station, and you'll get a ticket for

almost anywhere, with nothing to pay, if
you only say that they've carried you wrong.
That's about what you'd better do, to my
mind."

" Couldn't possibly," replied Helen.
" Don't know my way back in the dark, to
begin with."

" Dark, indeed! You'd have been more
welcome if you'd come by daylight," snapped
the old lady. " Funny time to call, this is.
Well, wait there," she added, closing the
door. " I must talk to the Doctor, I suppose. What he'll say, I'm sure I don't
know."

Whatever the Doctor may have said, the
library door was presently re-opened, and
Helen found herself in the presence of a
burly, curly, elderly gentleman with a rosy
face and a benevolent eye, who looked up
from the charity sermon which he was in

the act of preparing with the air of one to whom interruptions come as matters of course, and are disposed of as fast as they happen.

" Well ! What's the matter ? Lost your way on the rail—is that it ?"

" Yes, sir, if you please, I have lost my way. And I ventured to call here in hopes that you might be able to direct me to some proper lodging for the night. I was never here before, and I am alone. I really do not know what to do."

" Mrs. Nosegay," said the Doctor.

" Sir," said the lady.

" Leave us for a few minutes, if you please."

Mrs. Nosegay, by turning one ear to her master, and steadying the opposite eye upon Helen, seemed anxious to afford either party the opportunity of providing her with some

crumb of information to carry down-
stairs. But perceiving that nothing whatever would be said whilst she remained
in the room, she shook eye and ear into
their regular places, and retired in displeasure.

Doctor Orchard looked Helen rather hard
in the face—much harder and longer, indeed,
than she thought either necessary or gracious. Not, of course, that upon calling at
a strange house at half-past ten at night
you are to expect to be bowed up-stairs at
once to the best bed-room, but still the look
was one of something more than mere ordinary curiosity. There was, however, nothing for it but to confront it as best she
might, and wonder to herself whether they
could ever possibly have met before, and if
she was going to hear her own name pronounced directly.

At last, with a good-natured blink which was not exactly a smile, but the cheerful arrangement of countenance which comes over people who have solved a riddle, or made a good speculation, or otherwise brought intellect to bear to some purpose, he laid aside his pen, drew his arm-chair towards the fire, and said gravely and gently:—

"Tell me in two words why you are here. That is, if you can—if you please, in short. Don't be afraid. We will take care of you. Just give me something to say to Mrs. Orchard. Sit down, if you are tired. You shall have tea directly."

Helen could have burst into tears upon the spot. It was not the words themselves, but the kind, deliberate, powerful manner in which they were spoken, that upset her. She felt it impossible to prevaricate, and yet to condense a satisfactory answer into a few words was impossible.

"I had to quit my last place on a sudden," she answered, almost unconsciously. "Things happened which obliged me to leave. It was no fault of mine, I assure you. I have a very good character."

"Let's look at it," said the Doctor, holding out his hand.

"O, I didn't mean a written one," cried Helen, growing utterly bewildered; conscious that the fatigue and excitement of the day had been too much for her, and that she was betraying herself as fast as possible—"I meant——"

"I see! You meant a good conscience! Come, that's a better thing still. Well, we will take care of you for the night at all events. It happens luckily that we have a room vacant next Mrs. Nosegay's, and she

shall look after you. Mrs. Nosegay," continued he, as that lady reappeared with
marvellous rapidity in answer to the bell,
"this young person is under your protection
for the night. You will have the goodness
to make her very comfortable. I have
special reasons for these orders. She will
explain to me to-morrow enough to enable
me to forward her to her destination. In
the mean time, I have forbidden her to explain anything. She requires rest now."
And, with a courteous wave of his hand,
Helen found herself dismissed.

It is not to be supposed that any amount
of precept or exhortation would have bound
Mrs. Nosegay's tongue, or that under ordinary circumstances she would have gone to
rest, without such an account of Helen's
previous life and belongings as would have
done credit to the perseverance of a grand

inquisitor. Luckily, however, Helen was no sooner in the housekeeper's room, than Mrs. Nosegay made the startling discovery that she was 'a real lady.' Her hands betrayed her at once. Indeed she was no longer in the mood for masquerade, even if she had been enough of an actress to play out her assumed character with success. And this discovery, while it infinitely inflamed Mrs. Nosegay's curiosity, not only paralysed all attempt to gratify it in the usual manner, but made her so shy and obsequious that it was a relief to both parties when bed-time put an end to their conversation.

In short, Helen was shown into a tidy little servant's room adjoining Mrs. Nosegay's own dormitory, and, after all possible wants had been most kindly and carefully provided for, was left at last in peace and silence, to muse over the events of the day.

And the more she thought about them, the more unreal did the whole affair begin to seem. It appeared a week, at least, since she had changed her dress in the summer-house. The railway journey seemed an episode of very distant date; and the strangely considerate and even cordial reception which, in spite of her disfiguring disguise, had been so readily accorded, grew into an actual mystery before she fell asleep. Something in his manner towards her seemed to suggest that Doctor Orchard was influenced by other motives than those of mere charitable good nature—but the elimination of that something was a task beyond her power.

As a last precaution, she fastened the red leather pocket-book by a ribbon just below her knee, a little extra-careful device which perhaps I have no business to mention, but the wisdom of which appeared by its being found perfectly safe in the morning.

CHAPTER V.

"Sir," said Doctor Johnson, one day, "what a man has no right to ask, you may refuse to communicate; and there is no other means of preserving a secret, but a flat denial. For, if you are silent, or hesitate, or evade, it will be held equivalent to confession."

A nice lot of liars we should all make, if we gave in to this cool philosophy. But that some speculation of the kind ran through Helen's brain when she awoke next morning, and reflected upon the account which she would probably be expected to give of herself, is perhaps not the less probable. A change, however, in one respect seemed to be passing over her mind. Doctor Orchard's kindness had made a deep impression. A sense of the uselessness of all efforts at concealment was gradually growing up, as well as a sort of undefined consciousness that results were being taken out of her own hands.

So she dressed ; and, after carefully securing the pocket-book about her bosom, went down to Mrs. Nosegay's breakfast.

It was ten by the chime of the hall-clock before she received a summons to the library. Thither Mrs. Nosegay attended her, all civility, and with as much pride at having improved her costume into something presentable, as if she had been Helen's own waiting-maid.

The Doctor was there in his arm-chair by the fire, in just the same attitude, loose coat and slippers as she had left him in the night before. The same papers seemed littered upon the desk, and he was playing with the pen which she had last seen in his hand. It looked almost as if he might have forgotten to go to bed.

"Good morning!" he said, as Helen entered the room, fixing upon her as he spoke the same grave penetrating gaze which had disconcerted her the evening before. "I hope you have slept well and been properly cared for. Let us see now what we can do for you. There is no hurry at all; remember that. Remain here as long as you please. But, if you wish to leave us, let me know where you would like to be sent, and I will see to your being properly packed up and directed, at all events."

"I couldn't think of trespassing upon your kindness any longer, sir. Now that it's daylight, I can find my own way."

"Aye, but where? You came here last night lost on the rail. Where do your father and mother live?"

"I never spoke to a father or mother in my life," replied Helen. "I am alone. I told you so."

"But your friends? Don't resent questions. I must help you, you know. It is my duty."

"My friends obliged me to leave them; and that is my whole story. I am not going back to them at present. I choose to remain away."

"You choose to remain away! And you only eighteen last birthday," resumed the Doctor, with a more puzzled look than before.

" Eighteen," replied Helen, mechanically. It seemed almost superfluous to acquiesce. Doctor Orchard evidently knew all about her, if he only chose to say so.

" This is a sad business—very sad. I am not quite unprepared for what you tell me ; but we must consider what is best to be done. Excuse me if I leave you for ten minutes. I wish to consult Mrs. Orchard in the next room."

Thus left to herself, Helen had leisure to look about her. It was a handsome and almost luxuriously-furnished study, opening into a small conservatory. All around were massive book-cases, filled with evidently costly volumes, and what was particularly noticeable at first sight, quite an array of busts and heads—some of marble, some of plaster, which stared you out of countenance on all sides. The tops of the book cases were crowded with these silent effigies. Others, more honoured, were accommodated with private brackets ; while little knots of heads appeared to be conversing in all corners; and two or three, less favoured still, were evidently hatching mischief under the table. Some of them attracted Helen's girlish curiosity at once. They seemed to be faces which she had seen somewhere, and ought to remember. The sensation was not entirely pleasant.

It was upwards of ten—more than twenty minutes before the Doctor returned. " Come !" he said, re-instating himself in his arm-chair, " all is arranged. Nothing could suit better. Sit down now, and listen to me."

The same indefinable sense of power which had struck her the evening before, compelled Helen to obey like a child. She was to be

told what to do. In fact, she had found a
new master.

"You have a secret—a reservation," continued the Doctor, "which you probably wish
to keep. I don't ask it. I should not listen
to it at this moment. Whenever you deliberately wish for my advice, it shall be
yours. In the mean time, observe this.
I am a father myself, and indeed have
daughters much about your own age.
Whatever I should wish a man to do by
my own daughter, did she ever appeal to
him for aid in a difficulty, I will do by you.
You will be inquired after before long, I
have no doubt. In that case, I give you
fair warning that I shall exercise my own
discretion. I shall do just as I should wish
the man to do. Until then I intend to
place you in a situation of safety, where you
will be perfectly unmolested, and absolutely

out of the way of inquisitive people. Mrs. Orchard will explain all particulars, and convey you thither. To invite you to remain here would be against your own interest. We should only excite the curiosity of all Izzleworth. Tell me simply, that you trust yourself in my hands until further notice, and I shall be satisfied."

"I do, indeed, sir!" replied Helen. "I don't know how to thank you enough for all your kindness. As to my secret—that I will tell you with pleasure, at any moment. I would rather do so, I assure you."

"Tell it me when you find yourself perfectly free. Now let me take you to Mrs. Orchard."

"But—" began Helen, not knowing exactly what she was going to say, yet overwhelmed with irrepressible curiosity.

"But, what?"

"I beg your pardon, sir! But it is impossible to receive all this care and kindness without a sensation which I don't know how to express. I have had a feeling too, ever since I came into your house, that you knew all about me—every single thing. Do you really? You have not treated me like a stranger; and I can't understand it at all. It is like a dream to find myself received as if I had actually come by invitation. You won't mind my asking, will you? And how did you know that I was eighteen last birthday?"

"One must be a conjurer indeed, to guess that—mustn't one?" returned the Doctor, rubbing his hands and looking pleased all over. "Ha, ha! Your question delights me more than I can tell. Know all about you indeed! I wouldn't have had you miss this house for twenty pounds. No, my dear

young lady! Seriously, I am not only at
this moment in perfect ignorance of your
name, but I have not the slightest conception as to what part of the kingdom you may
come from. And, what is more, I know for
certain that, until last evening, I never saw
your face before."

"You know that!" exclaimed Helen,
amazed.

" Certainly."

This made matters worse than ever.
Doctors of Divinity are not supposed to
dabble in anything very deep—still less to
entertain familiars that 'peep and mutter;'
and this negative assurance, so confidently
given, sounded more like necromancy than
anything else.

" Now you puzzle me quite. I could not
say that myself of any face in the world."

" Neither could I, if you mean that you

could not speak so positively with reference to each and every face which might
come before you. But you're wrong, I'll
answer for it, in saying that you couldn't
do so with regard to any face. Look at me,
now. Did you ever see me before? Don't
think; but answer, yes or no."

Helen looked for a moment at that round
plump rosy countenance, that keen twinkling
eye, bold forehead, and firm good-natured
mouth, and replied, "No. Not at least
since I was a child."

"Very well answered. I don't suppose
you ever did. But if I wore the face of
Frederic the Great, for instance, the question
would have seemed ridiculous. You would
have answered that to have seen such a face
and forgotten it would be quite impossible.
There would be nothing to consider about—
nothing at all. Did you ever hear of the
great Philosopher of Zurich?"

" No, sir, never."

" What! Not of Jean Caspar Lavater ?"

" O yes. Of course I've heard of Lavater. He was a great phrenologist, wasn't he ?"

" He was the father of Physiognomy, the sister science. I am one of his disciples. Physiognomy has been my hobby, and I hope an innocent one, for the last thirty years. I am at last beginning to walk alone. All round the room you see my teachers. Lavater was right when he re-commended above all things the study of moulded busts. You can handle them, turn them, examine and measure them, entirely at your ease. That is your true education. Of course in this, as in every other science, infallibility is beyond our reach. We aim high, it is true, but at a point which fools only actually expect to strike. Neverthe-less, I can safely say that, during the last dozen years, I have been deceived in my first estimate of character from countenance very slightly and very rarely—never altogether."

"That does not make the matter less of a mystery to me," replied Helen smiling.

"There is no mystery about it! When one considers the astounding fact, that among the countless millions who swarm upon this earth, there are as many bodies as minds ; that there are no two human organizations precisely alike—certainly no two minds, and when we add to this that in our present stage of existence the mind can only act through the agency of the body, it is surely no extravagant conjecture that external difference of face and figure may have a certain relation—a necessary analogy to the internal difference of heart and mind. Is not this much more reasonable than to suppose that minds and bodies were distributed chance-medley? But we know that they are not. 'What treatment would that man deserve,' asks Lavater himself, with indignation, 'who presumed to assert that Leibnitz might have conceived the Theodicea in a brain like that of a Laplander; or that Newton might have balanced the planets and divided the rays of the sun, in a head resembling that of an Esquimau, who can reckon no further than six, and calls all beyond it, innumerable?' This, you will answer, is merely a question of power. Granted : but it is part of a principle. Come with me to Hanwell, and I will show you heads which never could have held a responsible brain. Come to Dartmoor or Portland, and I will point out skulls which couldn't possibly hold an honest one. These are simple facts, which all experience not

10—2

only warrants us in accepting, but forces
upon us, whether we will or no. Is there
then any clue to the nicer shades of character, as printed upon the outward face? Unhesitatingly we answer, yes. Every day's
experience convinces us that there is such
a correspondence. Every day, consciously
or unconsciously, we pass judgment accordingly. We speak of a good and of a bad
countenance. We say that such a face ex-
presses pride; of another that its owner
must be morose and peevish. A third we
declare looks sly, and a fourth benevolent.
One face talks to us of cheerful activity,
another only of brutal indolence. We could
trust one face : we doubt and detest the
next. And we are usually pretty much in
the right, at least, in the more marked cases.
Now, with this clue in his hand, who would
sit down contented ? What should we think

of the man who, having discovered that
there was sense to be extracted from a
hieroglyphic, and having actually deciphered
some half dozen lines, gave up all further
attempts as useless, and declared that the
rest was either unintelligible altogether, or
a mere blind string of casual crooks and
dots. The physiognomist does not stop.
He is not content with perceiving that one
particular face unmistakably announces
some special endowment—say sincerity, for
instance — without demanding why, and
tracing the same quality in others which to
a casual observer would indicate nothing of
the kind. Neither is he content to deal
alone with those qualities which are in
general more boldly proclaimed upon the
face. He reverses the process, and dissects
the lineaments of men remarkable for some
especial gift—wit, judgment, eloquence, for-

titude, or what not. He traces at last some line, some curve, some peculiarity of formation in lip or nose, eye or forehead, common to these men in their several classes. He recognises the same mark in a stranger, and spares no pains to discover whether, in his case, it announces a like possession; if so, he continues his investigation, until what was originally only conjecture, assumes the place of an established fact, and he can congratulate himself upon having added one link at least, to the noblest knowledge of mankind. This is a most vague, imperfect sketch of what we physiognomists venture to attempt. To indicate even the bounds and borders of our science, would be impossible in mere conversation. Even Lavater avowedly wrote only in fragments, and confessed himself incompetent for the finished task."

"I can't conceive how you could have formed any opinion about me, in such a moment," persisted Helen.

"The true physiognomist—the man who has learnt to grasp a face at all—decides always by first impressions. That is one of Lavater's golden rules. If I decide wrongly, it is not because I have been precipitate, but because I didn't understand my business. Never mind what I saw in your own case; I saw enough to justify me in acting as I did, and as I am doing. I told you just now, that I had never seen your face before. I could safely say so, because if I had, I should have considered it with interest—made a mental note of it, in fact. I should have liked to touch your head, too. Allow me to do so now. Will you look towards the window?"

"Ah, just as I should have expected,"

continued the Doctor, dropping his fingers upon Helen's brow, as if he had been striking chords upon a piano. "All firm and sound, and balanced well. Hey? what have we here? Acquisitiveness, I declare —and a little marked. Not run away with the family spoons, I hope?"

Helen felt herself blush and tremble. The red leather pocket-book which weighed upon her bosom, in more senses than one, might be enquired about after the next pat.

"No. I was just able to resist that temptation," she said, trying to evade further scrutiny.

"Ha, ha! Combativeness, I declare. I had not travelled quite so far down the parietal, but I'll be bound there's no mistake about it. Don't be affronted. Acquisitiveness is no bad point in itself; without it, no one can take care of their own, or

even enjoy their property. You'll ask me
next, why I didn't find out this by physiognomy. Well, we have two weapons : physiognomy, like the rifle, which strikes at a
distance. Phrenology, like the bayonet,
which we play with at close quarters, when
we get the chance. I should like to give
you my views upon the whole matter, but
that is impossible while Mrs. Orchard is
waiting. Come along with me, and in the
meantime, allow me to thank you for the
pleasantest ride on my hobby I've had for
I don't know how long! Stay, I forgot.
You have not told me your name, yet. Will
you do so ?"

Helen looked him in the face. Neither
could avoid laughing, as their eyes met.

" Yes ; that must be part of the bargain.
It is necessary that I should know it."

" I am Helen Fleetlands, sir."

"Thank you. The name is new to me. If you like to call yourself Miss Brown for the present, do so by all means. No one shall know who you are through me, unless with your own permission. Now, come along."

Mrs. Orchard, a nice, bright, bustling, little woman, received Helen with genuine good-nature, mixed with some slight shyness at the irregular nature of the introduction.

"You've had a good lecture on physiognomy, I'll answer for it, by this time! I don't know when I've seen my husband so pleased as when he came up-stairs last night and announced the discovery he had made. Well, he has made me promise to ask no questions, and you may be sure I don't want to ask any, but he is satisfied that you have reasons for wishing to remain cachée at present, and has himself arranged a plan which

I should hope would suit you perfectly. When the Doctor is satisfied, I am, of course; but indeed, there's no need to be a physiognomist in your case; at least, if there is, I'm one myself!"

"You are very kind," said Helen. "I have told Doctor Orchard that I am ready to explain to him at any moment, who I am, and how I come to be here——"

"O yes! But you mustn't explain to me! It would be as much as my place is worth to listen. You have no other clothes with you, I presume? I am obliged to ask the question."

"None at all. These are a disguise. I made them myself."

"Hadn't you better employ somebody else, next time?" asked the lady, laughing. "I am afraid we must change them for you. But I am forgetting what I was told to propose. Doctor Orchard, you must know, has a sister who lives some five miles from this —a sad invalid, poor thing. Her late companion was obliged to leave her suddenly, only last week, and she is miserable without one, and not yet suited. Now, Doctor Orchard thought that if you liked to go and stay with her for a week or so—in short until things took the right turn in your case, as I dare say they will before long, it might be pleasant for both parties. Any one whom her brother sends, Miss Orchard will welcome gladly. You will have no duties, except the attentions which one naturally pays to the afflicted. As to salary, you would of course resent the offer, so that the favour will be upon your side. There you will be perfectly safe and quiet, you see. Will you go ?"

"That I will, most gladly. It is the very

thing, above all others, that I should have wished for, had such a chance ever come into my head."

"Then we will lose no time. I could drive you over there; but that wouldn't do. Mrs. Nosegay is too provoking; and if she had the least idea that you weren't sent home again directly, we should never hear the end of it. What a pity it is that such chatterboxes were ever invented. Every chatterbox should have a regular lock, and some steady person to keep the key. That would be a capital plan, wouldn't it? No, I must take you in the carriage to the station. Then she'll think you've gone right away by train and forget all about you. I'll send the carriage home, and go on with you to Fell's Road, the first station out of Izzleworth, and we'll take a fly across to King's Woodlands; not much more than

a mile. That will do famously. And as to
dress, why we must borrow one from my
eldest daughter, which will fit you to a
nicety. Not that it matters much as regards Miss Orchard, for she's almost blind,
poor thing; but the servants would talk,
you know. And I must lend you a box,
mustn't I, or people would wonder. When
you get to King's Woodlands you can make
your own arrangements. By the bye,
Doctor Orchard specially charged me to
ask you whether you had brought any
money with you. You see his physiognomy
couldn't tell him that!"

"Plenty, thank you. Enough for all
possible purposes."

"That is well. Then suppose we start
in half an hour."

I have no occasion to lengthen my story
by giving you an account of the house in

which before luncheon time Helen found
herself fairly installed. It was simply a
neat, quiet cottage standing in its own
grounds, just within sight of the smoke and
spires of Izzleworth. Miss Orchard, several
years older than her brother, was, as Helen
had been prepared to find, a sad invalid;
almost helpless, and all but blind. From
Helen she required little, except the sensation of her presence; but the voice and
manner of her new companion struck her
instantly, and she sent word back to her
brother that he had found her a real trea-
sure. He must have been pleased I should
think with this additional testimony to the
value of first impressions.

And now in comparative solitude and
relieved from the fret and worry of Riverwood, Helen had time to turn her thoughts
inwards, and reflect upon what her life had

been—upon the strange position into which
she had so unexpectedly stumbled—upon all
that might be going on elsewhere, and upon
the future that was to be. Gradually, and
to her own infinite confusion, she recognized
the stupendous folly of which she had been
guilty in plunging unprotected and alone
amid the eddies of this extraordinary world.
Vague glimpses haunted her of what might
have happened had her drifting been less
providentially directed. And the very sensation of safety became so vivid and delightful, that when poor Miss Orchard wanted
her to promise to remain with her so long
as she lived, and offered to settle two hundred pounds a year upon her for life if she
would strike the bargain, she almost felt that
in devotion to this lone and ailing woman,
it would be pleasant to repay the great debt
of gratitude which she owed to her brother.

And then she thought of Riverwood
Lawn, and her grim old guardian and his
wife. It never crossed her mind that they
would have left England in her absence—
indeed the journey (I suppose for financial
reasons) had always been talked of as projected for her especial benefit. There was a
keen, malicious pleasure in picturing the
extravagant amount of wonder and confusion
which her disappearance must have created;
but, as days passed on, this reflection was
indulged in subject to one serious qualifica-
tion.

When young ladies are lost, people
usually think it worth while to advertise.
Helen was quite aware of this, and fully
prepared to be advertised for. Moreover,
she guessed, and correctly, that Doctor
Orchard would feel it his duty to watch the
papers upon her account. Every morning

she expected to see him appear with the *Times* in his hand, and to be obliged to re-count her whole story, in the hope that perchance he might be induced to regard matters from her own point of view, and not insist on packing her off instanter. But as day after day went over her head, and to all appearance no more notice was taken of her departure than would have been vouchsafed in the case of the kitchen cat, she became puzzled, impatient, and at last quite angry. It had cost her a great deal of trouble to manage her successful escape. And now it positively seemed that if she had ordered a post-chaise, and driven away in broad daylight nobody would have taken the trouble to remonstrate. This was very provoking: but furnished another reason for not going back in a hurry.

Long and earnestly too she thought of

Ferdinand, with the calm and happy trust-
fulness of a young and ardent mind which
has never known the pangs of doubt, or the
blight of disappointed love. She knew that,
for the time, correspondence was impossible.
But what of that? She was as confident as
of her own existence, that his heart turned
to her as faithfully as her own to him. A
few weeks more, and, come what might, a
grand revolution in her prospects must
necessarily take place, and their next meeting might not be so very far distant after
all. All was vague indeed and uncertain,
but there was a rosy dawn in the distance,
and she must bravely await its breaking.

Doctor Orchard, however, as time rolled
on began to wonder seriously. He could
make neither head nor tail of the business.
There was not the slightest doubt upon his
mind but that Helen was a young lady of

birth and position; and that her absence should apparently be treated with perfect indifference by those whose duty it was to care for her, was to him most unaccountable. The motive from which, as we know, the advertisement respecting her had been delayed very naturally never occurred to him. He searched files of all the London papers from a date a week at least antecedent to that of Helen's arrival, and continued his unsuccessful investigations day by day for a fortnight afterwards, when he gave up the attempt in despair. For some inscrutable reason she had been permitted to depart in peace. He was ten times upon the point of calling upon her to explain everything; but then the reflection occurred to him that after all he had no right to force her to gratify his own private curiosity. If her friends didn't choose to inquire after her through the ordinary channels, it was they who were alone to blame. She was perfectly safe where she was. He should be able to account for every moment of her time. Moreover, and irregular considerations of this kind will present themselves to the best constituted minds, it was quite evident that her presence was new life to his afflicted sister. No hireling either would or could have done for her all that Helen did, so cheerfully and gracefully every day. So Doctor Orchard at last resolved that, unless something were heard of Helen by a time which he fixed in his own mind, he would allow matters to remain as they were. When that period arrived, he intended to point out to her the necessity, for her own sake, of a full explanation.

In the meantime, having given up his daily search in the papers, the advertisement which gives its title to these volumes never attracted his attention ; and, but for an accident, the whole affair would have remained as great a mystery as ever, until the young lady herself thought proper to solve the riddle.

CHAPTER VI.

ONE morning, whilst looking out of the breakfast-room window at King's Woodlands, Helen was surprised to see the Doctor's great glittering black spatterdashes striding hastily towards the door. The Doctor himself was evidently plunged in thought, and carried a newspaper. There was no need to guess at what had happened. "Found, at last," thought Helen; "and a precious time they've been about it!"

"Well, my dear young lady," he said, taking Helen's hand between both of his own; "I dare say you have your suspicions as to what brings me here this morning."

"Well—yes;" replied Helen frankly, as she glanced at the paper in his hand. A sort of nervous sensation came over her for the moment; for, do you know that to read an advertisement respecting yourself is one of the most trying things in life. People really should think twice, before they advertise for one another.

"Ah, bother that paper! It's almost a fortnight old. I'm a dolt and a dunce—not fit for regular business of any sort or kind, I verily believe. But, come now, tell me this. You didn't happen to leave anything behind you at Bunnytail Station, did you? No trunk, parcel, bonnet-box, or anything else?"

"Certainly not, Doctor Orchard; and for a very good reason."

" Ha, ha ! Well, now I'll tell you how the whole thing came about. I chanced to be visiting among some of the small houses in Izzleworth, yesterday, when a poor woman, Mrs. Feltham, I think she calls herself, asked . me who the young lady might be whom she had seen in my wife's carriage a week or so since. At last I made out that she meant you, and then it all came out. She met you—that's her story—walking alone to Bunnytail Station. You travelled here together ; and you gave her three pounds when you parted, like a princess in disguise, which naturally made her wonder why you chose to cross the country third-class, instead of staying at home to ride your camel. Of course, I couldn't enlighten her upon that point, and I was at first really perplexed as to what I ought to do. I had neglected looking in the paper of late, because, to tell the truth, I fancied that for some strange reason or other your friends didn't intend to inquire after you in that way. However, upon going again to our reading-room to consult the file, this was the very first paper I chanced-to lay my hand on. Will you tell me whether that paragraph concerns you or not?"

We have réad the advertisement ourselves already. Here it is once more :—

"FIVE HUNDRED POUNDS RE-WARD! Disappeared lately, a YOUNG LADY, aged eighteen, of very distinguished appearance. She is slender and of middle height—dark hair and eyes—pale clear complexion, and is in manner peculiarly graceful and self-possessed. She had with her a very considerable sum of money ; but, it is believed, no personal luggage whatever. She was dressed, on leaving home, in a brown silk dress, purple cloth jacket, white straw hat, trimmed with black velvet, and grebe feather. Wore a curious oriental gold bracelet, plain gold guard-chain, and watch by Rosenthal, Paris. Whoever will bring her to Mr. Bloss, solicitor, No. 14, New Square, Lincoln's Inn, or give information leading to her recovery, shall receive the above reward. Thursday, May 1."

Helen read the passage from end to end, her colour heightening all the time.

"It must mean me, I suppose," she said at last. "That was the dress I wore. I know Mr. Bloss by name. I think he was my papa's solicitor, or had something to do with the property. But this is painful, Doctor Orchard—dreadfully painful."

"Not so pleasant as might be, I am afraid. Nevertheless, since I, who never had the good fortune to see you in a brown silk dress and purple cloth jacket, or white straw hat trimmed with black velvet, contrived to recognise the portrait at once, we must not quarrel with your description. Now, you know, I have only one course open. As a clergyman, a gentleman, and a father, I am bound to take the matter out of your hands. I do so from this moment. Mr. Bloss, whose name I see here, is, I suppose, a mere man of business. You have no fancy for being carried to his office, I presume?"

"Certainly not. Admiral Mortlake, of Riverwood, is my guardian. I left his house the very day upon which I arrived at yours. It is no use talking about reasons now, but I fancied that I had very good ones for acting as I did. I am perfectly ready to go back."

"Good," replied the Doctor, making a note in his pocket-book. "This, then, is the course which I propose. I shall write to the Admiral by to-night's post to apprise him of your safety, and accompany you myself to Riverwood to-morrow by the ten o'clock train. I do not ask your acquiescence; because, as I have already told you, I mean to relieve you of all further responsibility. But if you have any objections, let me hear them."

"I couldn't think of allowing you to take such a journey upon my account," replied

Helen. "I found my way here alone, and I can easily take myself back."

"But it is my duty not to permit it. Your having done a foolish thing once, is no reason for doing it over again. Besides, you said something to me, when you first came, about your friends having obliged you to leave them. A regular misunderstanding, I suppose?"

"I had better tell you the whole story, hadn't I?" said Helen. "I have often wished to do so, and I shouldn't be happy in leaving without letting you know all about me. I have sometimes wondered that you should never have asked."

"Hum! Perhaps not from want of curiosity. Tell me now, however. I shall be delighted to listen."

In as few words as possible, Helen told her tale; sufficiently, at least, to show what had been her leading motive in running away. "And now, Doctor Orchard," she exclaimed, as she concluded, "I am quite satisfied! Five hundred pounds! My goodness, what a sum to offer. O, I'll answer for it the Admiral must have been in the most dreadful fidget, before he thought of giving that much. Somebody must have made him do it; for he's a great deal too stingy to have offered it out of his own head. I really am quite delighted. There must have been the most famous to-do, and the whole thing will be cleared up now. Don't you think it will?"

"I hope that everything may turn out as you wish; but I am no lawyer, and do not sufficiently understand your position to offer any opinion. But, as regards your returning home alone, you must recollect one thing. This advertisement has been read, as you may suppose, by thousands upon thousands of people. Everybody in your neighbourhood must be on the qui vive, with such an immense reward in the air. You will be stopped before you reach Riverwood Lawn, as surely as you stand upon that rug."

" I see you are determined to claim the reward yourself," laughed Helen.

" Upon my honour, I think I deserve it a great deal better than the first clown you may meet; who will pounce upon you with a great whoop, and scamper away with you like a sack, making the whole parish ring with the noise of his good luck !"

" My good gracious me ! What a dreadful position to be in—to be liable to be taken up by anybody !"

" I am afraid it is exactly the position in which you have placed yourself. However, upon second thoughts, and after hearing your story, I believe it may be as well that I should not accompany you personally. I don't suppose I should be over-welcome, and it might almost look as if I came to have the pleasure of magnanimously declining the reward. No, I won't go; but I will do what will answer equally well. I'll send my gardener, David, along with you. He'll travel second class, so that you'll know nothing about him; but, in any emergency, recollect that you're in his custody by my written orders. When you reach home, send him to the right-about without ceremony. I think that will do."

"Dear Doctor Orchard, how very kind and clever you are! But, is it absolutely necessary that you should write beforehand? I would so much rather return unexpectedly if I might."

And then came out all Helen's little plan.

She had set her heart upon reaching the
summer-house unobserved, and there quietly
arraying herself in the identical dress which
she had worn on leaving Riverwood, and
which had been so graphically described in
the advertisement. Then she proposed to
walk boldly into the house, as if she had
never been away at all, and take her chance
of what might happen. She had no fears
as to the result. She intended to be a helpless ward no longer. 'Defiance, not De-
fence!' was to be the watchword of the
coming day.

The Doctor good-naturedly yielded. "You
shall carry my letter yourself," he said. "A
letter must be written. You have no idea
of the care which is required in matters of
this kind. You have no conception of the
awful forfeit which this prank of yours
might have demanded. Don't think of that

now; but submit to anything rather than run such a risk again. By the way, I quite forgot to ask—how about this 'very considerable sum of money,' which I see mentioned in the paper?"

"Ah, that was my folly. I did carry away some bank notes, and they have been the plague of my life ever since. I really did so out of the merest mischief. My guardian I felt had been wronging me for ever so long, and I thought it only fair play to frighten him out of his wits. Besides, I wanted my disappearance to make a great row; and I thought that every little would help. But the notes are quite safe. They are in my pocket at this moment."

"O dear me. The family spoons after all! Well, this only makes it the more imperative that no time should be lost, and no risks run. Remember that these notes are really a dangerous possession. I don't know that it ought to alter arrangements," continued the Doctor thoughtfully. "I don't know that it is my business to inquire further. But, for Heaven's sake, be very careful. You might be arrested at any moment upon a warrant for having them about you. I almost wish you hadn't told me this. Don't let us say any more about them. Get them out of your own hands at the first possible moment, whatever you do."

And the next morning saw Helen in the train. There had been quite a sorrowful parting all round. Miss Orchard was in despair, and would have doubled her late generous offer, if there had been any use in doing that. The Doctor felt as if he had been taking leave of a daughter; and Helen herself was conscious of a sense of disloca-

tion such as she could never have imagined
would have attended the severance of so
short an acquaintance. But partings are
the rule of this life; although we only
notice them when they are painful.

"Write to me when you get home," said
the Doctor. "Write at all events when
you get married. I must send you a sou-
venir. I think it shall be myself in white
wax. You didn't notice me, I dare say,
among the much better company upon my
book shelves?"

"Do send me your face, Doctor Orchard!
It shall have the very best place in my room."

"You shall have it. Physiognomy for
ever! People laugh at us physiognomists
—at us who see them through and through!
Don't forget David. He is in the next
carriage. Give me your hand once more.
Let us hope that we may meet again."

"We'll manage that much, some day, which is better than hoping. You shall have a good long letter before long. I am only so sorry I cannot stay upon Miss Orchard's account."

In due time the train arrived at the Bunnytail Station. Followed by David, who slouched after her at a respectful distance, ready however to do any amount of combat on her behalf at the shortest notice, Helen reached the outskirts of her guardian's territory, which she re-entered exactly at the same spot by which she had quitted it, more than three weeks before.

"Thank you, David," she said. "You see I am safe at last. You can tell the Doctor that you left me upon my own ground. I am vexed that I can't ask you to the house. But you'll find a little inn close to the station; and you'll have time to get some dinner before the next train." And dropping five shillings into his hand, she disappeared among the trees.

The cupboards were exactly as she had left them. Nobody had thought of searching the place, and the doors had never been unlocked. In ten minutes time her clothes were slipped off, and she stood dressed in exactly the same attire which she had worn on that memorable Thursday afternoon. Had Paul arrived a trifle earlier, he would have been too soon to catch her in that costume—perhaps too late to find her in the other.

Agitated as she was at the moment, his sudden appearance upset her altogether. A mist came over her eyes, and for an instant she fancied that Ferdinand himself stood before her. As she recognised a stranger, her heart after one sharp bound, seemed to waver and then stand still. She did not speak.

"Miss Fleetlands!" exclaimed Paul, unable to contain himself in his astonishment.

"You know me?" replied Helen, after an embarrassing pause. "Perhaps you were looking for me," she added, with returning composure.

"I have read an advertisement relating to you, Miss Fleetlands; and of course recognised you at once. I know perhaps more than I have any business to know," continued he, stammering and blushing like a schoolboy, "but I hope that you will believe that I am entirely at your disposal, and that you may implicitly count upon my services, should there be any which I can possibly render."

"You have been amusing yourself with trying to discover me, I suppose, ever since you saw the advertisement," retorted Helen, with sudden displeasure.

"Not with any sordid motive, I assure you, upon my honour. I am a gentleman —a barrister of Lincoln's Inn. I certainly amused myself, as you say, by following up the announcement which appeared in the *Times*, just as one might try to solve a riddle. Your name was then utterly unknown to me; and I had not even the remotest idea where you lived. It has so happened, however, that information has fallen in my way which leads me most earnestly to wish that I could serve you. My folly has already cost me dear," concluded Petersfeld, with a dismal recollection of the calamities of the past fortnight, "and if you tell me that I have now arrived too late, I not only take my leave at once, but with the solemn assurance that I will never mention your name again to any human being."

No one could possibly doubt the perfect

candour and sincerity with which these words were spoken. In fact, Paul's face was one which it was impossible to distrust, even without the practice and penetration of Doctor Orchard.

"Thank you," replied Helen, more graciously. "But I am upon my guardian's own grounds at this moment. In a few minutes all this will be over."

"You are aware, I presume, that the Admiral and Mrs. Mortlake are both abroad—"

"Abroad!" echoed Helen. "Is it possible that they should have gone without me? Are you perfectly certain of this? You must be mistaken."

"Perfectly certain," replied Petersfeld, delighted to find that there was some prospect of his being of use, after all. "They went abroad on the 17th of last month—the day after you left Riverwood, and have not yet returned. Some servants remain. Otherwise the house is empty."

"Good gracious, this is a nice business!" gasped Helen in dismay. "I'm really very glad that I met you. I wouldn't go home for all the world in their absence. I must go to Mr. Salterton at once. And yet that's just what I don't want to do. It would spoil the whole thing, and look as if I flinched at the last moment. Besides, it would not be right by him."

Naturally enough, she concluded that the servants left at home had, in all probability, received orders to detain her should she ever venture to return. That would be humiliating enough; but the unlucky pocket-book made matters a thousandfold worse. To have walked into the drawing-room, triumphant at her successful escape—triumph-

ant at having fulfilled her own time, and
returned of her own free-will, for all that
Scotland Yard and the *Times* newspaper
could do to the contrary; and finally, to
have flung the unopened pocket-book upon
the table, a splendid trophy of ingenuity
and magnanimity, combined, would have
been a grand beginning. But to be seized
and searched, and have it taken from her as
if she had been a thief—perhaps even to be
treated as one, was a terrible contingency.

"O, by the bye, I quite forgot to mention
one thing," suddenly exclaimed Petersfeld.
"You'll think it very strange, but the servants in the house yonder are all under the
impression that you are with the Admiral
and his wife on the Continent. I am perfectly certain that none of them have the
least suspicion that you are missing."

"Impossible!" cried Helen, opening her

eyes. "Why they must all have known of it directly I left home. There could have been no starting in the morning, and I not missed."

"I assure you, however, that it is the fact. I have not a conception as to how the business was managed, but managed it undoubtedly was. You know the St. Mark's Bay Hotel, I daresay. Mr. and Mrs. Maldon's."

"Perfectly."

"Well, I was staying there lately, and we talked about the Admiral, and the people at Riverwood, and both Mr. Maldon and his wife were confident that you had been of the party. From what I have heard, I have no doubt whatever but that by some clever ruse, effected for some particular purpose, a complete mystification was accomplished. Indeed, that was what first made me suspect

that something or other must be wrong, and
ten times more anxious than ever to get at
the bottom of the whole affair. I saw your
guardian myself in Paris, at the Grand
Hotel; and what do you think—he had not
only engaged a room for you, but had
actually procured your name to be posted
up in the bureau, as if you were staying in
the house. It's all part of some regular
plan, you may depend upon it."

Helen looked utterly bewildered. "I
think," she said at last, passing her hand
slowly over her brow, "I have some guess
as to what his motive may have been. I
fancy he may have been liable to get into
some shocking scrape with the Court of
Chancery, if it had been known that he had
lost me. If so, I'll answer for it, the fright
has done him good. At all events, I've had
travelling enough; though most assuredly,

I didn't get as far as Paris. If you are right in thinking that the servants suppose that all is as it should be, and that I am upon the Continent at this moment, I shall have the pleasure of undeceiving them. I shall go to the house at once. But one favour I will ask you to do me."

"Name it, my dear Miss Fleetlands!" exclaimed Paul, delighted beyond measure. "You cannot imagine the pleasure I shall have in being of service to you."

"It is an important service," rejoined Helen, half hesitating, "and you will see the perfect trust which I repose in your honour, directly I name it. I took with me, when I left Riverwood, a very large sum of money in bank notes—"

"Three thousand pound notes," interrupted Paul. "They were advertised for. I have the advertisement in my cigar-case.

It appeared, immediately after you left home, £150 was offered for their recovery."

" My goodness me !" exclaimed the young lady, "what a hopeless tangle the whole thing is, to be sure. However, since the notes were all the time in my pocket, the one advertisement was of about as much use as the other."

" Just as much."

" Well, then, what I want to say, is this. I have the notes about me at this moment. Now it may be quite true that the servants at Riverwood have been deceived, as you say ; but I'm confident that there must be some one or other about here who knows the whole story. Depend upon it, there is some one on the look-out for me upon the Admiral's account. It is inconceivable that it should be otherwise. Well, I wouldn't for the whole world have these notes found upon me, and taken away, as it were, by force. That would be too ignominious. Nobody shall hand them over to the Admiral except myself, or some one by my authority. Would you mind taking charge of them for me, for the present. Then I shall feel quite safe, and ready to brave and bear anything. Will you do it?" continued Helen, producing the pocket-book. " I feel that I can trust you, although I do not even know your name."

" I will do anything in the world you please," replied Petersfeld. But this is, indeed, a great piece of confidence to repose in a perfect stranger."

" I must trust somebody," returned Helen, impatiently. " I can't have this thing about me any longer, and I won't carry it into that house, as matters stand. Take it— please do! and give me your address to write to, when I want it again."

Paul produced his card. "There is my name," he said, smiling. "You see the Albany is my London address, but I am staying in this neighbourhood for the present. I will write down the name of the place."

"What! Are you staying with the Bunnytails?" asked Helen surprised.

"You know them, do you?"

"I know the farmer as a neighbour. I know his wife by sight. How do you come to be there?"

There was evidently a compliment conveyed in the question, and Paul congratulated himself that he had not been indiscreet enough to trust to the farmer's promised hospitality, and offer Helen a shelter at the Bottom.

"I am there quite promiscuously at present. Mrs. Bunnytail has a sister who married Mr. Buttermere, a member of our bar. I chanced to meet them one night at dinner at his house, and only yesterday I encountered the farmer at St. Mark's who induced me to pay them a visit. Mrs. Bunnytail is not fascinating."

"A fat, odious woman. Insupportable, I should think. But you will take this pocket-book, will you not? Don't think me very rash and foolish. I have been studying physiognomy of late."

"It is very good of you to accept mine. Fortunately, as perhaps you are aware, these notes are stopped at the bank, and owing to their amount, mere waste paper in my hands for all practical purposes, so that I shan't be tempted to run away with them."

"Ah! I remember hearing my guardian ask for their numbers, and all that sort of thing, when he received them. Thank you very much. They can, I think, cause you no trouble, since no one except myself can possibly know that you hold them. How long do you remain with the Bunnytails?"

"Until I hear from you," replied Petersfeld gallantly. "My time is at my own disposal. Will you send me a line at any moment when I can possibly be of use? I don't know whether I could help you as a lawyer. To tell the truth, it's just about the only capacity in which I don't think I could. But at any rate, do let me have the satisfaction of thinking that you would send for me in any emergency, as some atonement for my folly in pursuing an enterprise with which I had nothing whatever to do."

"If I find myself in distress, I will send for you, Mr. Petersfeld!" replied Helen, gaily. "But I shan't be killed and eaten up, at any rate, until the notes are forthcoming. Now we must part," and she held out her little hand.

As Paul grasped it with all the earnestness necessary to explain his complete devotion to her interests, there was a low rustle among the neighbouring yews. Some one was passing close by; in fact, the back of a black coat was indistinctly visible.

" What's that, Mr. Petersfeld ? That was not a dog."

" No," said Petersfeld, and started in pursuit.

He was much quicker than the intruder, whoever he was, but the latter knew the ground, and dived through clipped hedges, and dodged round statues, in a way which gave his pursuer no chance.

" I have lost him," said Paul, returning discomfited. " But I am sure I know the man. You were quite right, Miss Fleetlands, in suspecting that there was some one on the look out for you, upon the Admiral's account. I have seen that fellow lurking about for ever so long. His name is Tobacco. He has gone in the direction of the house. Will you go there now?"

"Yes. I am in for it, and can take care of myself, now that my pockets are empty. But I shouldn't mind if you would be good enough to see me safe indoors."

Gladly Petersfeld accompanied her within sight of the garden entrance, and was rewarded by the display of unfeigned astonishment with which the housemaid who opened it, recognised the apparition of her young mistress.

He had been right in his conjecture. It was Mr. Tobacco himself who had vanished so concisely. From the tap-room of the 'Six Bells' he had observed Petersfeld leave

St. Mark's the evening before, in company
with farmer Bunnytail, and thought there
could be no harm in looking him up on the
following day. And when Paul set out
upon his afternoon stroll, Mr. Tobacco accompanied him at a wary distance, delighted
to find that his progress, although capricious
and irregular, and enlivened with an occa-
sional pipe, tended steadily in the direction
of Riverwood Lawn. He watched him
enter the grounds, and to his intense amaze-
ment, beheld the meeting which took place,
and which he naturally considered must
have been deliberately planned and precon-
certed. He could not manage to creep
sufficiently within earshot to discover all
that passed, but he ascertained enough for
his own private purposes. To have attempted to arrest Helen under such formid-
able escort, would have been downright

madness. To have been detected among
the bushes might have led to a thrashing.
So he crawled off at a critical moment, in
hopes of getting away unnoticed altogether.

How Petersfeld got back to Bunnytail's,
I don't suppose will ever be explained. His
brain seemed absolutely on fire. He had
found the lady of the advertisement. He
had touched her hand, looked in her hazel
eyes, and been rewarded by her unbounded
confidence. What would he not have given
for another interview, to have heard from
her own lips the whole strange story !
Whither had she been ? Where had she
passed those many mysterious days ? And
then, her beauty. It was like a bright wonderful dream. Never, he thought, in his
whole life-time had he beheld such loveli-
ness. To be sure he might have recollected
that faces seen for ten minutes—seen too

under the influence of overflowing excitement, and which look appealingly and imploringly into your own during the interview, are apt to leave rather a radiant photograph behind.

If he could only have exorcised that malignant Captain out of the story—blotted his name from the Army List, or hurled him—like an anachronism—a hundred years either backwards or forwards, what would he not have given for the opportunity. Then, indeed, his adventure might have a really magnificent end. And why not, yet? No game is ever lost till it is won, and he hugged the pocket-book in the breast of his coat. I don't suppose he would have parted with it for the full value of its contents, honestly paid over a bank counter in sounding gold. They must meet again about that!

Nothing, I suppose, in the way of marked success ever befals any of us unaccompanied by some sort of chastening. In Petersfeld's case it was vexatious to remember that, just as the prize was actually within his grasp, he should have made up his mind irrevocably to abandon the pursuit as wild and useless. Again, it was annoying to reflect that after all his trouble and exertion, he might have gone home disappointed but for the chance occurrence of a meeting, brought about by no dexterity of his own, and against which the odds an hour before would have been incalculable.

But these are reflections in which nobody has any business to indulge. Ask any man who has toiled through life with some grand aim in view, and stands at last upon the very pinnacle of his young ambition, two plain questions. Ask him, first, whether he

never wavered in that unfaltering perseverance of which he is now so ready to boast
—never confessed to his own soul that he
had attempted too much, and that nothing
remained but to knock under, and tell me
if his answer be not that the chain of resolution which drew him at last to his appointed summit, was many and many a time
dragging loose along the road.

Ask him again, whether he could ever
have risen as he rose, unless for some unexpected and extraordinary opportunity which
never entered into his calculations when he
went forth in his morning strength, fresh in
his untried fearlessness and faith, and tell
me if he does not answer, No.

In fact, I suppose, we all ride our several
careers pretty much like men in a cavalry-
charge. Each has his own horse's head to
mind—his own weapon to manage; and be-

yond that a good deal takes place around
him over which unfortunately nobody in
particular has any control. And when at
last the survivors gallop in, clear of the
smoke, one with a standard in his grasp—
one with a foreign major kicking at his
saddle-girths, and another with lost lance
and broken bridle, why nobody cares to
understand how it happened that one came
so much better out of the encounter than
another, and the question is not argued when
it comes to the distribution of medals.

Paul returned to Bunnytail Bottom just
in time for supper. It would have been
difficult to have reached it when feeding of
some sort was not going on in the way of
breakfast, luncheon, dinner, tea or supper, to
say nothing of intercalary snacks.

In the excitement of his late adventure,
he found that to conduct himself like a quiet

average person, was impossible. There was nothing for it but either to shroud himself in primeval silence, or allow his overcharged mind the escape-valve of reckless merriment. And the latter, in a social point of view, appeared the least objectionable alternative.

The farmer and his wife were overjoyed. " Well, Paul," exclaimed the lady, " this does one's heart good only to hear and see ! This is just as it should be, my dear. Ah, you've been hankering after Linda all the afternoon. Anyone could tell that. And the more you hanker, the happier you'll grow, and the heavier you'll wax, and the more you'll eat and drink."

" Aye, I'll be bound you're hearing truth, nephey," struck in the farmer. "Feeding's everything, to us and all mankind. And it's begun to tell upon you already. Lord, if you'd only tell me how to fetch some of

my beasts yonder into condition as quick as
we're fetching you, I'd hand you a couple of
pounds apiece, any day. I would, indeed.
Drink some more ale, nephey. It'll make
you thrive. Why, one would think you'd
lived all your life long on crackers and
water-cress ! Now you see what it was you
wanted—don't you ? Why Lindy won't
know you again. She'll say you're somebody else ; and—ha, ha !—object to marry
anybody except the lean gentleman with his
gizzard out of order. Happy thing we met
at the 'Six Bells,' wasn't it ?"

After supper, Mr. Bunnytail proposed that
they should smoke their pipes till bed-time,
a motion which was ably seconded by his
wife, who considered that it had a marked
bearing upon the question of punch. And
when the latter element of enjoyment had
been mixed and ladled, she gave herself up

to eloquence and imagination, and showered down blessings enough upon Paul and Linda to have lasted them during their joint lives with a comfortable provision over for the survivor.

Just as her good humour was at its height —her husband in a state of placid narcotism, and Petersfeld pretending to listen, but in reality unconscious whether she was addressing him in Greek or English, there came a modest knuckling at the door, and the slut of all work gingerly entered the room.

" If you please, mistress, there be a gen'l-man's servant at the front door as is enquiring after Muster Petersfeld, saying as how he has a messuage to convey to him, if you please."

Paul started so conspicuously as to attract the notice both of host and hostess.

" What's this, Paul, and how now ?" exclaimed the latter.

"I suppose I had better go and find out," returned Petersfeld with assumed indifference. "Tell the man to wait, my good girl, will you. I'll come presently."

"Where does he come from? Ask him that," cried Mrs. Bunnytail, before the maiden could close the door. "And ask him what he's come about—mind you do!"

"I understood him to say, mistress, that he was a gen'leman's servant up at River-wood Lawn—" the damsel was beginning, when Petersfeld peremptorily interposed.

"Pray, Mrs. Bunnytail, allow me to receive my own messages," he said, with forced composure. "You see you compel me to go to the door at once. How can I tell what he may wish to say to me?"

"Go with him, Bunnytail," exclaimed the lady. "I don't like these solemn, secret messages hovering headlong in at this time of the night, I do assure you. What Paul knows we're bound to know. Get up, man, and go."

"Mr. Bunnytail knows better, I am sure, what is due to a guest," observed Paul, looking for his hat. He was terribly afraid that some absurd attempt might be made to prevent his quitting the room.

The farmer, however, smoked on. "No use, madam. Leave nephey alone. Let him see the young man in peace and quiet. And, when he comes back, let him tell the holy truth, and hide nothing."

A respectable-looking person was waiting at the hall-door. "Mr. Petersfeld, I believe?" he said, touching his hat, and producing a letter.

"Yes—yes! I am Mr. Petersfeld. Are you from Riverwood?"

"I am, sir. I have a private message for

you from Miss Fleetlands. Might I take the liberty of asking you to come a few steps away from the door. There is a female at that window, and what I have to communicate is of importance."

"Hang that woman! I wish she was at Jericho," thought Petersfeld. "Yes, my good friend, you're quite right. Come along. Now we can't possibly be overheard."

"The message, sir, was respecting the pocket-book which Miss Fleetlands delivered to you this afternoon. Probably you may not have it at present about you?"

Paul, without answering, clutched instinctively at his breast-pocket. "Well, what about it? Why do you ask? Tell me what the message is. Stand still, can't you! We're not marching to London."

To his horror, he became suddenly aware that a second person was silently accompanying him upon his right. A glance backwards told him that he was guarded by two men behind.

"What's the meaning of this!" he shouted, and was instantly seized on all sides.

" We have our warrant, sir," said one of the men, turning on his dark lantern, and producing a paper. " You are our prisoner. You must come. We have a coach waiting in the lane."

"Come! Where?"

" Ha, ha, ha!" crowed Mr. Tobacco.

" Get on, men," said the Inspector with the lantern.

CHAPTER VII.

PERPLEXED and mortified to the last degree by the signal failure which had attended all attempts to recapture his ward, Admiral Mortlake quitted Paris, and, purely from a nervous desire for change of scene, visited Rouen. But Rouen gave him no rest; and, a few days afterwards, he moved northwards to Dieppe.

Thence he wrote to Mr. Clover, stating his fixed determination not to return to England until Helen was found, or until his presence there became otherwise absolutely indispensable. Annoyance had made him

14—2

morose and obstinate, and Helen would, I
am afraid, have been rejoiced to learn how
plentifully she had repaid Mrs. Mortlake, at
second hand, for the miseries of a bleak and
bitter childhood.

One morning—the very next I believe
after the tragic termination of Paul's last
evening at Bunnytail Bottom—a waiter
skipped in upon him while shaving with a
telegram in his hand.

" Depêche Telegraphique, Monsieur
l'Amiral, s'il vous plait! Tenez M'sieu.
Depêche Telegraphique ! Bonnes nouvelles,
M'sieu ! V'la !"

Telegrams are not usually very long; and
the one in question was very short.

" Clover to Admiral Mortlake, Hôtel des
Quatre Saisons, Dieppe. Cross at once.
Letter at P.O., Newhaven."

In a towering passion, and with a mixed

sensation of curiosity and dismay, the Admiral obeyed this imperious summons, and the following is a copy of the letter which he found awaiting him :—

> "New Square, Lincoln's Inn,
> "May 16th.

"MY DEAR ADMIRAL,

"I regret very much the being obliged to summon you home in so abrupt a manner, and at so short a notice ; but a most unfortunate circumstance has occurred. The Lord Chancellor, a short time since, seems to have received information that you had left England for the continent, taking Miss Fleetlands with you. As to who his Lordship's informant may have been, or with what view the intelligence was furnished, I can form no conjecture. However, as your solicitor, I received a summons yesterday from his Lordship to attend him at his private room. His Lordship did me the honour to observe that he considered the removal of Miss Fleetlands beyond the jurisdiction, without previous leave, was, under existing circumstances, a most flagrant and aggravated contempt of court; and that he should require you to attend personally before him, within forty-eight hours, and produce the young lady; or deal with it, upon your return to England, in the most marked and summary manner.

" The Telegram which you received was sent by his Lordship's direction. It was, of course, impossible for me to leave his Lordship under a misconception, or to conceal the true state of the case. To have attempted anything of the kind would have placed me personally in a most dangerous position, and could have answered no useful purpose so far as you are concerned.

" I regret to say that his Lordship ex-
pressed his grave displeasure at the course
which we thought it right to adopt; even
taking into consideration our belief that the
measures directed to Miss Fleetland's recapture seemed to promise almost certain and
immediate success. Deferring further explanation until we meet, I will only add,
that the whole affair has caused, and is
causing me the deepest uneasiness. I most
earnestly beg that you will not fail to attend
at Mr. Bloss's chambers, New Square, to-
morrow, by three o'clock, when I will meet
you, and accompany you before the Lord
Chancellor. It is, I fear, hopeless to expect
that, in any case, you will be permitted to
retain the guardianship of Miss Fleetlands ;
who will probably be handed over to Mr.
Salterton, as the successor to that office
appointed by her father's will. Her con-

tinued and unexplained absence, after the search which has been made, and the extravagant reward offered, is the most extraordinary circumstance within the whole course of my practice.

"Trusting that you will believe that, in a most critical and delicate conjuncture, I have acted, so far as my own judgment went, with every possible desire to study the interests of yourself and your ward, and assuring you that such has been the case, I remain, my dear Admiral, in great haste,

"Yours faithfully,

"HARRY CLOVER.

"ADMIRAL MORTLAKE,

&c., &c.

"P.S., P.S.!—I reopen my letter with the greatest pleasure. I have this moment (11 p.m.) received a telegram from St. Mark's. Your ward has returned to River-

wood, and the notes have been discovered
upon a Mr. Petersfeld, a member of the
Chancery bar! It seems probable that he
received them from her as an innocent
bailee; at least, Mr. Bloss, who is acquainted with the gentleman, inclines to
that opinion. I shall run down to Riverwood at once; but will return in time to
keep my appointment as above. Please,
don't fail to attend."

Poor Mr. Clover! He was evidently
alive at last to the fearful extent in which
he had so unwarily committed both himself
and his client.

Let us leave them to make their peace,
as best they may, with the Lord High
Chancellor. I have another, and more interesting letter for your perusal.

To my great surprise, as I recognised
Petersfeld's handwriting in the direction to

myself, I noticed that it bore the Southampton post-mark. It was a scrawled and
hurried epistle; scarcely legible in many
places. Printers, however, can read anything: so I shall send them the original
and see what happens.

> "On board the Jura,
> "Southampton Docks.

"MY DEAR WORSLEY,

"That confounded lecture on energy,
which you were good enough to read me, a
fortnight ago, has been my ruin—absolute
ruin. When I think over all the mischief
and misery I have got into in consequence,
I scarcely know how to keep my temper.
Much you care about that! But, just look
at what you've done. Here I am, actually
engaged to be married—at least I'm supposed to be so—a thing I can't possibly
undertake, especially after what's just hap-

pened. How it will end, I haven't a notion.
If it would be any consolation to old Buttermere to shoot at me, he'd better do it at
once. He won't have the chance after to-
morrow. Then I've been in prison, and
stood in a dock, and been actually addressed
as 'Prisoner at the bar.' Nice way of making my first appearance in that direction,
wasn't it? I expect, too, that I'm liable to
be pulled up for contempt of our confounded
Court, into the bargain; but I shall not
stay for that. I can't face Lincoln's Inn
again, at present. Reflect a little upon all
this, next time you feel inclined to moralise,
and find yourself in want of a victim.
When you read these lines, I shall be on
my way to Egypt.

"The last part of my story is briefly this:
I went back to St. Mark's-on-the-Sea; and,
as ill-luck would have it, fell in with old

Bunnytail. You may recollect him at
Buttermere's dinner, the other night. He
enticed me over to his farm-house—of which
I need say nothing whatever—and the very
first thing I did was to walk across to
Riverwood, and fall in with Miss Fleetlands
herself! What do you think of that?
Wasn't that a triumph, after all my trouble!
How about energy, now? Yes, we met at
last; and, by Jove, I don't know how to
regret, after all, having done what I could
for such a creature. I won't try to describe
now; but you never in your life saw such a
countenance. One of those faces that makes
you feel wild at first sight and ready for
anything. Well, she asked me to take
charge of those —— bank-notes for her.
You may fill up the dash as you like : I am
sorry to say I didn't leave it for the amount.
Of course, like a donkey, I took them at

once and carried them off to Bunnytail
Bottom. Shall I ever see that face again?
—Never, I am afraid. I don't know what
should take her into Egypt.

"That very evening I was coaxed out of
Bunnytail's by constables—taken into custody, and spent the night in the lock-up at
St. Mark's. The police were civil enough.
Civil indeed! I declare I'm going mad.
I wonder whether the lion at the Zoological
consoles himself with the reflection that
people don't chaff him, and compassionately
shy old bun. They told me I was in for
being accessary to a felony, and should have
to go for trial. They'd no doubt about that,
they said, because I'd been seen about the
place for ever so long, and a fellow of the
name of Crackleton—I think I told you
about him—the manager of the bank there,
was on the bench, and determined to make

an example of me. I have the comfort of believing that he will be hanged without having had that gratification. I will make an example of him, and a mummy too, if I catch him walking about Egypt.

" Next day I was escorted to the justice-room. They didn't take me before the bench at once. I don't know why. I don't even know whether Miss Fleetlands was there. I fancy she was, but I didn't see her. The police told me that my case was on, and I complained that I thought it a great deal too bad, if I was only going to be brought in to be sentenced. ' Well,' they said, ' that did seem rather hard lines, didn't it?' and that was all the consolation I got. At last I was asked for, and placed at the bar. The chairman—to do him justice—told me that I stood there only for form's sake. The charge of felony, he said, had been withdrawn by leave of the bench, and that being so, the charge against myself, as accessary, of course fell to the ground. I was no longer in custody. I might depart whenever I liked, and I instantly resolved to go to Egypt.

" I should, as you may suppose, have called at Stone Buildings on my way, but to tell the truth, I was too horribly afraid of encountering Buttermere. So being utterly hard up for cash, I drove straight to Jonah Molochs, in Golden Square, and got him to come down with one hundred pounds on the security of my furniture, etc., at the Albany. I had to leave him my key, with authority to put a man in possession. I don't like it, however, and I wish you'd see him soon, and make it all square. I've written to the governor at home for a couple of hundred, and I dare say he'll send it.

I've asked him to forward it to you, upon
my account. He never minds much about
money when he thinks I really want it.
Only screws a little now and then, to induce
me to try and make it myself. As to making
it at Lincoln's Inn, that's out of the question, now, so he'd better brush up his
Juvenal and say :—

> ' Accipiat te
> Gallia, vel potius nutricula causidicorum
> Africa, si placuit mercedem ponere linguæ!'

I suppose he will be alive to the unlike-
lihood of my realising much income in
that direction. Fancy anybody green in
Egypt!

"Another thing: I wish you'd look in
on the Buttermeres, and try if you can't
smooth matters down a little. I should
think that you might. The whole thing is
the most absurd and extraordinary blunder

I ever heard of. I don't take the entire blame on myself, because if Linda hadn't chosen to mystify me at her father's dinner about the Riverwood business, there wasn't the ghost of an occasion for anything of the kind. If she has taken a fancy to me, I'm very much flattered, and very sincerely sorry. But what put her up to talking as she did, I can't for the soul of me imagine. In short, barring an unlucky mistake I made, in putting a bank-note intended for my tailor, into a wrong envelope, I really consider that I'm the lamb and not the wolf, and shall console myself with this reflection in Egypt.

" You'll think me, I dare say, a great fool for going. I can't help that. To face people in England at present, is utterly impossible. Merely to cross the Channel would be called skulking ; but everybody is satisfied at once, when you tell them that a fellow's gone to Egypt.

"I shall write to you again from the first place we touch at—Gibraltar or Marseilles. You'll have to do a few little commissions for me, and send them out by the next mail. If you will take that trouble, you may consider it in the light of a small set-off against having sold me into Egypt.   In the meantime,

"Yours very resentfully,

"PAUL G. PETERSFELD."

"John Worsley, Esq."

Within ten minutes after I had finished this highly Egyptian epistle, I was on my way to the Waterloo station.   There was a train to Southampton at a quarter past nine, which would arrive about noon, and in the faint hope that I might not be too late to do some sort of good, I started at once.

As to inducing him to give up his project, that I feared, was hopeless. But I did not like to lose the chance of verbal remonstrance against such utter folly, for it is easier to talk than to write to people who confess to seldom reading a letter 'right through,' and make a point of destroying it upon the spot.

I had never been at Southampton before in my life, except once in a night passage to Havre, so that the place was altogether new to me. Making my way to the water-side, I hailed a sturdy, weather-beaten individual with a monkey-jacket and tarred hat, who was hitching himself hither and thither in that persevering and inimitable manner peculiar to Jack ashore.

"Has the Jura sailed yet?"

"That's her: over yonder; with Blue Peter flying. Hauled out of dock this

morning, first thing. She's just about off,
I reckon."

"Shall I have time to get on board?"

"Well, you may and you mayn't, you
see. All depends upon the mails. That's
what she's waiting for. Directly the mail-
boat ranges alongside, and the Agent gets
his mails on board, she's off. Wouldn't
wait then not for the whole royal family
putting off in the port-admiral's barge. If
you want to go aboard, I should say it's
now or never."

"Can you tell me where I shall find a
boat?"

"I'll show you," said that ancient mari-
ner good-naturedly, shuffling away at an
astonishing pace. In two minutes I found
myself seated vis-à-vis with a couple of
strong fellows, pulling with might and main
—stimulated by the promise of an extra

half-crown in case they reached the ship before the mail-agent.

It was a glorious morning. Amid one broad universal blaze of sunshine, the crisp waves leapt and glittered. The water was alive with craft of all descriptions, and as we neared the Jura, towering over all, the joyous roll of her band, playing

'In the days we went a-gipsying,
A long time ago!'

made the whole thing seem like some grand party of pleasure. But there were bursting hearts and weeping eyes on board the Jura, for all that. The crowd and confusion was something wonderful. Shore-going people were being seriously admonished of their boats alongside. Leave-takings were going on in all directions. Sheep and pigs, ducks, and cocks and hens, were more plentiful than even at Bunnytail Bottom.

I walked forward at once, knowing it to

be a matter of conscience with all young
Englishmen, the moment they find themselves on board a steamer, to hurry to the
bowsprit and fill their pipes. As I expected,
there was Petersfeld, seated on a hen-coop,
and offering biscuit to a chicken opposite,
with as much composure as if he had been
bound for Greenwich, with nothing more
serious than champagne and whitebait in
prospect at the end of his trip.

" Hollo, Worsley !" he exclaimed, starting
up. "My good fellow, what upon earth
brings you here ? Did you get my letter ?"

" Of course I did. Were you in hopes
that the postman would make a mistake ?"

" What a fool I was to post it last night !
I didn't mean you to have had this trouble.
I thought we should have been off hours
ago. My good fellow, I hope you haven't
come down upon my account ?"

"But I have come upon your account, and, what's more, I have a boat to take you back again. This ship sails in ten minutes. I tell you candidly that I shall write you down a fool if you sail in her. What business have you here? Do you mean to throw away all chances of work, annoy your people at home, and get yourself called 'eccentric' into the bargain — about the most damaging adjective a man can have tacked to his name? Nonsense! Come down the side with me. I've read your letter. I understand your feelings perfectly. And I'll undertake to satisfy you that I am right in what I now call upon you to do. Recollect the success you have just achieved. I declare, when you first started, I should have liked to give a hundred to one against your doing what you actually did. It would be a real disappointment to me, now, to see you throw away your chances, without giving yourself fair play. Come along. By Jove, here's the mail-steamer actually alongside."

"My dear Worsley," replied Paul, grasping my hand, "I dare say you're quite right. I'd take you're advice with pleasure, if I possibly could. But I can't. I can't face Buttermere. I can't face the men at Lincoln's Inn. I can't indeed, after all that has happened. Besides, look here. That's my ticket for Alexandria — just cost me thirty pounds down. Can't afford to throw that into the sea, you know," concluded he, with a forced laugh. "Thank you a hundred times for coming. I shall always recollect it. But, I say, you'll be too late. Hark!"

A clear hearty voice, distinct above all the bustle, suddenly shouted,

" Gun !"

There was a flash and a bang. A cloud of silver smoke went whirling overhead in the sunshine. Fluttering down from the mast head came a small blue and white flag. The band stopped dead in the middle of a polka ; and, after a moment's pause, struck up the National Anthem.

The voyage had begun.

" Hullo, Governor, we thought you'd given us the slip," said my boatmen. "Another half jiffey, and we should have had to cast off without you."

CHAPTER VIII.

WHEN a castle of cards four stories high comes tumbling flat upon the nursery table, there is something in the suddenness and completeness of the disaster which makes even a good child ready to cry. A great deal of pains has been taken—a great deal of ingenuity exerted. Little fingers have been anxiously moistened—lips compressed —and eyes curiously peeped through, as the bright pagoda rose up square and tall. In one moment, all is over. Time and pains and trouble have all been thrown away. The tower is a thing of the past. There is

nothing to show for it—absolutely nothing.
Buttress, wall, and pinnacle, all are gone.
Not a trace of their existence, not a vestige
of identity need be looked for in the fallen
pack.

I felt much in a child's mood myself, as
I returned from Southampton. I had taken
a good deal of trouble, and put myself to
no slight amount of professional inconve-
nience, in order to make the journey. Ten
minutes on board the Jura had been sufficient to send me home again. And what
had I done? Absolutely nothing. I might
just as well have been in Court. Petersfeld
was gone, and to attempt expostulation upon
paper was—as I well knew—perfectly useless. A confused feeling that I had some
share of personal responsibility in the matter
of his going abroad, annoyed me. An idea,
however, occurred while in the train, which

I put in execution directly I reached Stone Buildings. I wrote a note to Buttermere, and sent it across by my clerk. This was what I said :—

"MY DEAR SIR,

"Petersfeld left England for Alexandria by P. & O. Steamer to-day. I knew nothing of his intention until I received a letter from him this morning, when I immediately started for Southampton, in hopes of bringing him back. Unfortunately, my journey was unsuccessful. I now venture to ask if you will allow me to have an interview with your daughter, upon the subject which we discussed the other day at your chambers. I should not make this request without good grounds, and I believe you know me well enough to trust to my discretion. "Yours faithfully,

"JOHN WORSLEY."

The reply was immediate.

" DEAR WORSLEY,

" I was hasty and inconsiderate upon the occasion to which you refer, and you have a right to every amends in my power. Linda shall be prepared to receive you in my study in Harley Street to-morrow afternoon at five. Will that hour do? I have the most perfect confidence in your honour and discretion, and shall not expect her to communicate one syllable of what may pass. Should she wish to do so, it is understood that I am at liberty to hear everything.

" Yours truly,

" F. BUTTERMERE."

I was, of course, punctual. My visit had evidently been arranged for, as I was ushered

at once and without a word, into a small
untidy room upon the ground-floor, furnished with two chairs, and an immense
table littered with books and papers. A
pair of great, shaded lamps, like genii of
the apartment, stood sentinels over the
green-baize. Rakes of lamps they looked,
accustomed to sad hours, and to wink and
blink, and pledge one another in cannikins
of midnight oil, long after all the household, except its laborious master, were warm
in bed.

In a few moments Mrs. Buttermere, accompanied by Linda, entered the room. I
will not do the former the injustice of saying that she seemed very doubtful as to the
propriety of my visit, and perfectly certain
that I had acted most audaciously in pro-
posing it. I had only a general perception
that such was the case; perhaps as intui-

tive upon my part as it was politely veiled upon hers.

"Mr. Buttermere tells me that you wish to see Linda alone," she remarked, after the usual common-place observations. "Shall I leave you together? You will not be disturbed here, and you will find tea in the drawing-room when you have had your say. Linda, you must bring Mr. Worsley upstairs."

"Mr. Buttermere was good enough to allow me a moment's interview with Miss Buttermere," I replied, "and with her permission, I will avail myself of your kindness, before joining you in the drawing-room."

"O, by all means. I understand nothing of the matter, but Mr. Buttermere's wish is quite sufficient." And with these words, rather dryly spoken, the lady quitted the room.

I have seldom felt more keenly shocked than when I looked at the poor child before me. O that this should have been the little sparkling coquette of but a few evenings ago. The pretty form—the delicate features —the rich auburn hair impatient of its tiny bonnet—these were all there; but there was pain and misery written all over her countenance : there was nervousness and almost terror in every quick movement of her gloved hands.

"We have just come in from driving," she said; "I hope you have not been kept waiting ?"

I perceived that she spoke because she could not help saying something. The excitement of the moment was unendurable. I would have given anything to have known how best to soothe it. I could only do my best.

" I have not waited a moment. I have only just strolled down from Lincoln's Inn. I believe, Miss Buttermere, that I am here to take a great weight off your mind; at least, I sincerely hope so. I am here, at all events, upon the part of a friend of mine, to offer you the most submissive apology which man can make for having made your papa very angry, and yourself, I fear, very unhappy, by one unfortunate act of incaution. If he were not at this moment probably somewhere off Finisterre, I would bring him here to plead for himself."

" O, no, no, no, Mr. Worsley. It is I who have done wrong. It is I who have made myself unhappy. It is I who have spoilt my whole life, and learned what real misery is at once and for ever. It is I who ought to ask his forgiveness;—it is, indeed. You don't know all, I am sure."

" Pretty nearly so, I believe. It began with a conversation about a certain Miss Fleetlands, at your papa's dinner table."

" Yes—yes. At least not exactly. I had made a most foolish wager with my sisters —I did not know how very wrong it was— and I led him to suppose that I knew something about that young lady. In reality I knew nothing—only her name. I had happened to learn that by the merest chance. I have never ventured to say a word about this either to papa or mamma; it would have made them so dreadfully angry. And a day or two afterwards he wrote me a letter, and sent me a bank-note. I could not quite understand the letter; but I felt certain that the money was never intended for me."

" You were quite right. The twenty pounds was intended for his tailor. He put it into your envelope by mistake. It is just the sort of thing he is always doing."

Linda fairly sobbed. "I see it all now. I see at last what I have done. O, why did I ever go to Mrs. Springletop! She is a friend of mine, you must know, Mr. Worsley; and, as misfortune would have it, I went to her to talk about the letter. I wanted advice, in short. Well, she persuaded me that it could only have one meaning, and made me lay out the money on an emerald snake-bracelet, and write and thank him for it, and so on; and so it all came about. Oh, how dreadful it seems now. Is there any hope —any help for me, do you think?"

"My dear Miss Buttermere, these little contre-temps happen every day. We will put yours to rights at once. Your acquaintance with our friend Petersfeld was, at all events, a very short one."

16—2

" There was no acquaintance at all! That was what made the whole thing seem so frightfully shocking. But, say what I would, I was always met by the same answer, that I was only a child, and that it was lucky I had people about me who knew how to manage affairs. I am so thankful to think it is all over. Will you take back the bracelet? Pray do. I will fetch it directly."

" You shall give it me presently. He would of course wish you to keep it; but I agree with you that it had better be returned. That is the right course. And now, one word upon my friend's behalf. He is in such perfect despair at the annoyance which he has inflicted upon you, that he has actually left the country, and is at this moment upon his way to Egypt. He has thrown up his chances at the bar—probably incensed his relations; and will most certainly never come back until he feels that you have forgiven him."

" Forgiven him, indeed! He must forgive me first ; or, rather, let me forgive and forget myself, which I can never do."

" Upon my word, I never had such an impracticable pair of penitents to deal with in all my life! You're just as bad as he is. You both tell me you can't forgive yourselves, so I advise you to try what happens after forgiving each other. However, I shall now know what to say to him when I write by the next mail. Now, my dear Miss Buttermere, I took the liberty of asking for this interview in order that this foolish entanglement might be cleared up to yourself in the first instance. I was quite right you see. If Mr. or Mrs. Buttermere had known of the very innocent little trick which brought it all about, a good deal of trouble might

have been saved. Everything must now be
explained to them, and you may take my
word for it that they will be intensely relieved upon learning the whole truth. There
really is nothing to be angry about, which
is rather a pity, after all the fuss that has
been made. Have 1 your permission to tell
the whole story to your father?"

"Papa has just come in," gasped Linda,
in a choking voice. "I heard his footstep
in the hall."

"Capital. Then we will get the business
over in no time. Allow me for one moment
to assume the freedom of an elder brother,
and beg you to ask him to join us."

"Well, Worsley," he said in his old cordial tone, yet looking fagged and worn to
the last degree, "is the consultation over
already, or am 1 called in to assist? Can
you give us any new light upon the subject
—hey?"

"I hope so, at all events. You will scarcely believe what a ridiculous little blunder lies at the bottom of the whole affair. Your daughter will explain it all; but, before she does so, let me say one word. You remember, doubtless, an evening when I had the pleasure of dining with you, not very long ago. We talked, if you recollect, of a young lady whose mysterious disappearance had just been announced in the *Times*, and for whose recovery five hundred pounds reward was offered."

"To be sure we did. I remember the advertisement perfectly. It made Brindlebun quite curious. What then?"

"Petersfeld was at that moment engaged in trying to find her. He had taken up the pursuit simply upon seeing what we all saw in the paper. He had been in Paris, upon that very business, during the morning of the day when he was last in this house."

" What on earth had he to do with her ? What do you mean, Worsley? Are you going to make him out *non compos?* no brains—not accountable for his actions ?"

" My dear sir ! He has found her."

" The deuce he has !" exclaimed Mr. Buttermere, as if using up his last ounce of breath. " Went to work and found her, did he ? Most extraordinary thing I ever heard of."

" I say the same. And now, to save Miss Buttermere the trouble, I will try to explain how, in the middle of his hot pursuit, he managed to commit the most unlucky mistake which has caused so much annoyance both here and to himself."

Step by step the confession was accomplished. Buttermere took his seat upon the table, between the lamps, and listened with knitted brows.

"So that Mrs. Springletop, confound her, was at the bottom of it all! I almost guessed as much. And the bank note was never intended for Linda?"

"It was intended to pay for trousers. He was writing to his tailor at the moment, and put the bank note intended for him into the envelope addressed to your daughter. That's the whole story."

"Upon my word, Worsley, I thank you very heartily for all this. What's done, can't be undone; but we shall weather it somehow, I suppose. And so Petersfeld has gone to the Pyramids?"

"Gone, in despair of ever being able to show his face again in London. I have just asked your daughter to send him her forgiveness; but, I tell you candidly, I don't think even that will bring him back."

"Well, it's all a pity. The whole thing

is such a joke, if you look at it only in one
aspect, that it's hard not to be able to laugh
at it. Write to him, Worsley, and tell him
to come back. And so Linda really took
him in—this clever fellow who found the
lady at last! Upon my honour, the whole
thing is most extraordinary. But there is
no sting about it now. We must manage
to rub through. It will only be a nine days'
wonder, after all. These things happen
every week—eh, Worsley? If one could
only box Mrs. Springletop's ears! But as
for you, darling, don't fret. It wasn't your
mistake. And Worsley, I shake hands with
you, and thank you with all my heart. We
shall rub through somehow. It was a mistake altogether, from first to last. Mrs.
Buttermere and I must talk it over. And
as you said just now, Worsley, it will only
be a nine days' wonder, and we shall rub

through perfectly. Yes, darling, it was all a mistake—a silly stupid mistake of people who ought to have guided you better. We are all right now. We won't be too hard upon poor Mr. Petersfeld. Don't let him catch cold on the Pyramids, Worsley. You have done us all a service to-day; and, so far as he is concerned, the past is dismissed, and we hope that you will tell him so."

That self-same evening a letter, which you will never read, followed Petersfeld to Alexandria by the Marseilles mail, and an emerald-headed snake slept in an iron box on the topmost story of No. 9, Stone Buildings, Lincoln's Inn.

Let us return to Helen.

Everyone, I suppose, must remember certain passages in their lives which have left behind them the impression rather of a sort of nebulous mist, than of a series of separate events, connected, yet distinct. Some rush of circumstance, unexpected and overwhelming, has blended things in one perplexing maze, and we shrink from the task of dissection, as from something laborious, long, and hopeless.

Something of this sort was the case with Helen after her return to Riverwood. A few facts only stood out solid and certain, against a general back-ground of confusion.

Mr. Bloss himself reached Riverwood the day after her arrival, charged with the mission of bringing her up to town. Upon this occasion it appeared that her presence before the Lord Chancellor was indispensable. Mr. Salterton accompanied them. As her guardian next in succession, it was rightly considered that he would do well to be upon the spot, to accept the office which would probably at once devolve upon his hands.

Of Helen's meeting with the Rector, you must forgive me if I do not speak. Something of its purport you may, perhaps, presently learn. He was kind—for he never was otherwise. He was loving—for Helen was to him as his own daughter. But let the interview itself remain within the veil. It tore Helen's heart to think of, afterwards. The mere recollection was like a rending of the very roots of pain. She was, at last, conscious how grave had been her fault— how blind and inexcusable her folly. But she is now in the train, and upon her way to London.

It was the first time that Bloss and she had met since the day when he received her —a little Indian baby—in Southampton harbour, and escorted her to the very station

from which they were just departing.
Events since then had indeed run their
mysterious round; and one may imagine
the interest with which the jolly old gentleman surveyed his fellow passenger. The
latter, upon her part, listened with the deepest interest to much that Mr. Bloss had to
tell. He could speak to her of her own
papa, when a bright and curly boy. He
could talk about the making of the will—
penned by his own hand—which had
brought him wealth in his dying hours;
wealth, alas, too long delayed. He could
say something about her Indian birth-place,
as it had been described to him by his cor-
respondent of the firm of Joy, Jingle, and
Jump, and amused her with a description of
her own tiny self, as she first opened her
eyes in his face, upon the deck of the mail-
steamer.

"O, by the bye, Mr. Bloss," she said, after these topics had been at last exhausted, "I wonder if you know Mr. Petersfeld, the barrister of Lincoln's Inn. I am afraid he got into sad trouble about the bank-notes which he was so kind as to take charge of for me, and I was really grieved. But that, I hope, is over now. You cannot think how kind and considerate he was. I really almost wish that I had wanted his assistance—he seemed so burning to give it."

"Ho, ho, ho!" chuckled Mr. Bloss. "My dear Miss Fleetlands, it's a capital story, and I ought to have told it you before. Yes, I do know Mr. Petersfeld; and, what's more, I am indebted to yourself for the honour of his acquaintance. You may well look surprised. Never was such a droll affair known since the world began. When your guardian, the Admiral, thought it right to advertise for you, he chose, as you know, to put my name in the paper, as the person to receive you in town. He pitched upon me, you understand, as being the person who first brought you to his house; independently of which there were reasons for wishing that his own London agents should not appear in the matter. Had they done so, the chances were that inquisitive people—clerks especially—would have put two and two together, and your name been discovered and blazoned right and left in no time; and this, to do him justice, he spared no trouble to prevent. My own name you see afforded nobody any clue whatever. Well: the very morning that the advertisement appeared, who should march into my office but Mr. Petersfeld himself, just as I was in the middle of my luncheon. 'Give me full particulars of the

young lady, Mr. Bloss, for I'm going
straight away to find her, as sure as you sit
there!" That was what he said, or something like it. To tell you the truth—it was
our first meeting you must remember—I
doubted whether his head would ring quite
sound if one tried it; but he came with the
card of a very good friend of mine, Mr.
Worsley, and upon his account I really told
him all I dared. As to his finding you, the
idea never once entered my mind. And
that you should after all have encountered
each other in the strange way you did, just
at the critical moment, is almost more than
strange. Of course he might have claimed
the reward."

"Is it paid yet?" inquired Mr. Salterton.

"Paid! Lord bless you, no! We shall
have claims from half a dozen quarters.
When the detectives abandoned Riverwood,

they left an agent of theirs, a dirty little
understrapper of the name of Tobacco, to
keep a look out upon their account. He
seems to have put the Riverwood constabu-
lary upon the scent, as to the notes at all
events. Of course he will stand out for his
own. I have had other notices already. It
is quite exceptional, in a case of this kind,
to find the reward pass peaceably into one
pocket."

"I feel quite certain that Mr. Petersfeld
would have nothing to say to it," remarked
Helen.

"Not he! Oh, dear, no," chuckled Mr.
Bloss. "Not in his line at all. But now
you mention his name again, it reminds me
of another most singular fact. One never
knows exactly how these things get wind,
but I had this from the very best authority.
Just fancy. Since his visit to me—that is

to say while in full pursuit of yourself—he has managed to snatch a hasty moment to get himself engaged to one of the prettiest little girls in London—a daughter of one of the magnates of our Chancery bar !"

"Nonsense :" exclaimed Helen, laughing. "That was really making use of spare minutes, which, somebody says, is such an excellent habit. What is her name—her christian name, I mean ?"

"O, Linda,—Linda Buttermere. I have admired her often, at her papa's dinners. Charming little girl, indeed! Really Petersfeld is a most remarkable young man. Never knew anything like his energy. One doesn't know what he may not do next. I shall send him a good heavy brief, I know, before he's a week older !"

"Linda,—what a pretty name !" And, for the next thirty miles, Helen, with her

usual impulsive generosity, was considering
what wedding-present she should choose for
Paul and Linda, as some acknowledgment
of the debt which she felt she owed to the
former.

London was reached at last, and Helen
conducted to a private Hotel in Cork Street.
Thenceforth, for the next two days, all
seemed mist and confusion. There was an
interview with the Lord Chancellor, during
which she was seriously taken to task, and
punished with a lecture of which she too
painfully admitted the wisdom. And there
was a formal reconciliation with her guardian, which took place in his Lordship's
presence. It was not a very gracious affair;
but neither party could be expected to feel
quite at ease. To her great relief, nothing
whatever was said in her presence about
the notes, which had, as a matter of

course, been lodged at the Riverwood Branch
Bank.

And now, resisting all temptation to en-
cumber my story with technical minutiæ,
I will only add that the conclusion of the
business was as follows: Admiral Mortlake was ordered to pass his accounts—pay
certain costs—and hand over Helen to Mr.
Salterton, who was appointed guardian in
his room. Riverwood Rectory was to be
Helen's future home.

CHAPTER IX.

"I HOPE, Mr. Salterton, it is understood that these rewards are all to be paid out of my own money; and that the Admiral is never to be troubled about anything which he has received upon my account," said Helen, a few days after she had taken up her abode at the Rectory.

"That must be an after-consideration, my dear. For the next three years, the power to bind or to loose lies neither with you nor me."

Three years! A desperately long time it seemed, all things considered. Could it be possible that they had indeed to be faced. Sad or unprofitable they need not be. And yet, years of discipline and penance Helen knew that she had deserved. Wisely and bravely she resolved to submit with patience,—to trust to the endurance of a love which was all in all to her in life,—and, in the meanwhile, by genuine and unfailing cheerfulness, to make Mr. Salterton rejoice that he had found a daughter. The only hope to which she permitted herself to cling was that, some day or other, long perhaps before the three years were expired, the prohibition against letter-writing might be relaxed or withdrawn. That was the real sting of the separation; and, to her, it seemed an unjust, a needless, and a cruel measure. She could not understand why she might not at least be allowed to correspond with Ferdinand. If either she or he

had been actually in prison—regular con-
victs at Pentonville—that indulgence would
not have been forbidden. However, there
was no help for it. She felt that she had
much to be thankful for. Mr. Salterton
was always delightful; and in his sister, a
quiet, ladylike person whom she had scarcely
more than known by sight in the years
during which the Rectory had been forbidden ground, she began to discover the mak-
ings of another friend.

Indoors, there was work in plenty. Out
of doors, Camilla neighed from her stall.
She had of course accompanied her mistress.
Gigoggin, alas, was not there to attend her,
and sadly the old fellow was missed. One
would naturally have supposed that, after
his conduct in the matter of Helen's hunting-field flirtation, the Admiral would have
sent him about his business in no time.

But Gigoggin had lived at Riverwood almost as long as his master, and was not to be parted with upon a single quarrel, however serious. So master and man fought it out between them, and matters went on as before. The latter, we may be quite certain, would gladly have followed Helen to her new home; but the Admiral was obstinate and inflexible. Not in that way, at least, should Gigoggin, with his consent, enjoy the reward of his duplicity. And, without the Admiral's formal acquiescence, Mr. Salterton was firm in his refusal to allow the matter even to be discussed. It was a great sorrow to Helen, who, independently of other, and more recent considerations, entertained a sincere regard for the old friend of her childhood. But, like severer troubles, it had to be borne.

So broke the morning of what appeared

to be a new era in Helen's life—an era of
quiet probation, and of hope deferred. Misty
and doubtful in its dawning, how immeasure-
ably distant appeared its close!   Would she
ever live to behold that hour—to see matters
finally at rest—the ravel of her life at last
combed out smooth and even!

Never, in wildest dream of the night,
came a glimpse of the plan by which the knot
was to be so swiftly, so instantly disentangled.

One morning, scarcely three weeks after
Helen's arrival, a large old-fashioned carriage
drove up to the Rectory door. A tall, elderly
gentleman, of military air, with a white
moustache and a golden-headed cane, gravely
alighted, and was ushered into the Rector's
study.

"My dear Lord St. Margarets, is it possible that I have the pleasure of seeing you
again!"

" You not only see me, Salterton, but you see me with a favour to ask."

" A new sensation, I should think, if you are in earnest. Am I to take my pupil back again ?"

" Why, no. I am not clear that I should trust you with him a second time," replied Lord St. Margarets. " What do you say to his late escapade ? I suppose you have heard the particulars."

" I have, and with infinite concern. Of course, in one's own heart, one finds every excuse for a lad of his high spirit and perfect courage, with such a girl as Helen before him. But that he should have rushed right into the jaws of the Chancery Lion, is upon all accounts to be regretted. I was rejoiced to hear from himself, however, that he was not, in any sense, acting in defiance of your wishes—in fact that he had some reason to suppose, that, had he succeeded, you would not have been seriously displeased."

"Quite right. Quite true. He has acted towards myself, thank God, with the most perfect honour and good faith. I have not a word to say. Indeed, I take a great deal of the blame upon my own shoulders. I have lived too much for myself, Salterton. I have not held for him the position in the county which I might and ought to have done. But that is not the question now. Never having had the pleasure of Miss Fleetlands' acquaintance — never, in fact, having beheld her in my life—the match was not one of which I could be supposed to be personally desirous. My relations with the Admiral, her guardian, were far from cordial, and I could not help feeling that Ferdinand might, after all, be acting upon impulse, without the consideration which an affair of such extreme importance demanded. Still, I was so anxious not to appear to thwart him at starting, which is worse than useless in matters of this kind, that I fear I left him in a position which was only too likely to end as it did."

"Perhaps we have not seen the end yet," suggested the Rector, easily. "It is highly important, upon Helen's account, that I should be precisely aware of your views and wishes. That her heart is entirely fixed upon Ferdinand, I am certain ; and that she will, if necessary, wait with patience and courage three years and longer, I know quite well. But, since she has been in my house, we have never exchanged a syllable upon the subject. I felt bound, in the first instance, to learn the aspect in which you regarded the match ; and I only deferred writing to you upon the subject until you should have

had time to hear from Ferdinand upon his
arrival out, and matters had cooled down a
little after the late hurly-burly."

"My own views, Salterton," replied Lord
St. Margarets gravely, "may depend much
upon your answer to a question which,
amongst other things, I came hither to put.
I am come, as I told you, to ask a favour;
but the question comes first. If my son has
done a foolish thing, I am afraid your ward
has shown herself more than his match.
You will appreciate the circumstances under
which I now ask you to tell me the whole
story of her disappearance and return. I
give no credence whatever to rumour; and,
except from rumour, I have heard nothing.
Let me understand, first, what we may suppose to have been her object in leaving
Riverwood."

"To avoid remaining under the same roof

with people who had treated your son so scandalously," replied the Rector. "Helen was indignant, and with some reason. I was away from home at the time. They were upon the point of starting for the Continent; and the poor child, with nobody to appeal to, was, I verily believe, afraid of their company."

"Good," observed Lord St. Margarets, with deliberate emphasis. "You will agree with me, Salterton. The way in which they kidnapped Ferdinand was simply scandalous. I am aware that it was merely done to gratify an old feeling against myself. But she did well to distrust them, after that. I admire her spirit. But the world will ask for more."

"More is at their service. Helen left home at five o'clock on the afternoon of the sixteenth of April last; and, from that moment

to this, not one half hour of her time is unaccounted for. She travelled direct to Izzleworth in company with a Mrs. Feltham, a
parishioner of St. Mark's, whom she had
met near the station. On her arrival at
Izzleworth, she very sensibly enquired for
the clergyman of the place; and by the
greatest conceivable good fortune, if we are
to call it by no worthier name, found herself
at once in the house of Dr. Orchard, the
vicar. Orchard is a well-known man. He
was some years my senior at Balliol, but I
remember his name and fame very distinctly.
A little crotchetty, and given to physiognomy, or some humbug of the kind; but
true and honourable to the back-bone. Fortunately the Admiral has had the good
feeling to enclose to me a letter of his,
describing the events of Helen's stay with
him, and the sensation of love and admira-

tion which she contrived to excite in his family. I will read it to you at once, if you have no objection."

"Good again," repeated Lord St. Margarets, at the conclusion of the letter, "and there you will agree with me, Salterton. Upon my honour, I like her better than if she had stayed at home. In fact, my good friend," continued the ex-ambassador, subsiding into a diplomatic attitude, "I consider that this episode in her life may be at once consigned to oblivion. Are we so far agreed?"

"In so far that we may so consign it— yes. But not she, poor child. I felt it my duty to point out to her, in all gentleness, the greatness of her error, and I assure you I was frightened when the thing broke upon her as a reality. Her distress was agonizing."

"What a pity. Come, Salterton, I am ready to say the word. Give me your honour that she is the person to make Ferdinand happy:—you know them both."

"I give you my honour that, in my opinion, he will never meet with any one as likely to do so. More than that, I tell you plainly, Lord St. Margarets, that if he loses Helen, he will lose one in ten thousand."

"Good! I consent. You may tell her that at the age of twenty-three—she is nineteen, or nearly so, I think—I shall with pleasure receive her as the mistress of Saintswood, and retire upon Grosvenor Square. Tell her that my mind is quite clear upon that point."

"At the age of twenty-three?" repeated the Rector, musingly.

"Twenty-three, of course. You don't

seem satisfied, Salterton. Isn't that the age specified in her father's will?"

"Otherwise her fortune goes over? And the Court would of course listen to no proposal which might endanger one penny of it. Yes, I believe you are right. But my dear Lord St. Margarets — you are in earnest, I know, in your consent—is there no possibility of abridging this deplorable—this, I must say, shameful loss of time and youth to both parties? Five years! Must they really wait five years? Is it possible that these, the best years of their lives, are to be consumed in satisfying the injunction of a Court of Equity? Could anything be more preposterous? If we are to be ridden over rough-shod after this fashion, why not call things by their right names, and have a High Court of Iniquity at once?"

Lord St. Margarets never laughed. But

18—2

sometimes, when he was really amused, a curious smile would break at his lips, and then travel quietly all over his countenance before it disappeared. It came and went, upon this occasion.

" Why, yes. Five years is a long time to wait. I am not defending the system; but it exists, and there is only one person in existence who could strike off a single day."

" You mean the Lord Chancellor?"

" Most certainly not. Neither the Lord Chancellor, nor Guy Fawkes, nor anybody but yourself. I told you that I came here with a favour to ask. I am now ready to ask it. What do you say to consenting that the marriage shall take place, say a couple of months hence, just with notice enough in fact to make proper preparation?"

"Have I really any such power, my dear Lord?" exclaimed the Rector, jumping out of his chair.

"Certainly. I half suspected that you might have found it no part of your duty as executor to read your testator's will. Avail yourself of the chance now! Here is the copy with which I persuaded my solicitor to furnish me."

"God bless me! Why, of course you are right. Admiral Mortlake's veto has no longer any effect. How could I have been so stupid as not to perceive the fact!"

"As not to recognise yourself as reigning guardian?" replied Lord St. Margarets with a smile. "The king is dead—long live the king! Well, in that capacity, I ask your consent."

"Stay one moment. Surely my consent as guardian will not have the effect of annulling the injunction which is at present hanging over your son?"

"It will not. But upon our joint application to the court, I understand that it will be dissolved as matter of course."

"But, how as to Ferdinand? It is hardly a month since he sailed. Are you about to summon him back at once?"

"No need. He is at this moment in Grosvenor Square."

Mr. Salterton returned to his seat. "No more guessing upon my part, Lord St. Margarets. I cannot afford to be surprised at this rate. Will you explain?"

"The explanation is most simple. Fortunately or unfortunately, Ferdinand chose to go into a fever on the voyage out. I am not certain but that he was sent too soon— before, in fact, he was fit for travelling, but I suspect that other things may have had

more to do with it. Be that as it may, he
was landed at the first port touched at, and
the military authorities there sent him back
by the next transport. They said it was
his only chance. He is now getting all
right, thank Heaven. I had ambitious
dreams for him once; but after all that has
happened, I am content to see an augury in
this last occurrence, and to accept it as the
appointed termination of his professional
career."

"And you have said all this, Lord
St. Margarets, without even seeing
Helen?"

"Why, yes. I do not intend to be told
that I was myself the victim of fascination.
I believe in her good looks, and for the rest
I trust to you, Salterton. You have known
her from childhood, and I am satisfied. It
seems to me that Ferdinand's mind is quite

clear upon one point, and that's the great thing. Now you may introduce me, if you will."

Helen had just come in from a gallop upon Camilla. You know how she looked upon these occasions, and though recent events had stamped her features with a trace of care and sadness, they had perhaps given even more than they had taken away. Without the slightest guess as to who the stranger might be, she felt fascinated by his commanding air and stately presence. Wonderingly she allowed him to take her by both hands, and look tenderly down upon her fair young face. She stood bewildered under the clear gaze of those calm gray eyes, and the curve of that silken white moustache.

" You do not know me ?" he said.

" I do not, indeed," replied Helen. " But

your face is not strange to me. At least, I think not."

"It will never be strange, I hope. I am Ferdinand's papa. He has asked me to be yours."

Huzza!

At last we sail within earshot of wedding bells. Let us not linger now.

❋　　❋　　❋　　❋　　❋

"Helen," said Ferdinand, as they slowly walked their horses, side by side, beneath the waving branches of a summer wood, "I have a surprise for you to-morrow. Whom do you think you will see?"

"That I cannot possibly guess! There are so many people in the world."

"Your friend Petersfeld will be at Saints-wood this evening. I made a point of calling at his chambers, when I was in town yesterday, to thank him for his kindness to you. He is really a thorough good fellow. Of course, we fraternised immensely, when I reminded him that we had both gone to jail upon your account."

" You didn't bring that to his recollection, I do hope," cried Helen, colouring. " It is not a reflection which I am fond of, I assure you. What did he say?"

" Quoted an old Agamemnon chorus, which I perfectly recollect Salterton trying to drive into my head—called you

' Τὰν δορίγαμβρον ἀμφινεικῆ τ' 'ΕΛΕΝΑΝ!'

I hope you appreciate the compliment. Τὸν δ' ἀπαμειβόμενος, I asked him to come down to Saintswood and stay for our wedding; and, now I think of it, he shall be my best man. That will be a capital climax to his adventures, won't it?"

" Capital! It was very kind of you to

invite him. I shall be delighted to see him
again."

"You must know that he has been half
over Egypt, since you saw him last."

"Egypt! Impossible."

"It is a fact. He only returned last
Monday."

"Well! as Mr. Bloss remarked in the
train the other day, his energy is something
extraordinary. I feel certain that he will
become a very great man."

"There is no doubt about that."

Let me interrupt the conversation for one
moment. Whether or not my own letter to
Petersfeld had any effect in contributing to
his rapid return, I do not know. Probably
another, which he received by the same
(Marseilles) mail from his father, and which,
consequently, reached him a few hours after
he landed, may have had more to do with

it. The old gentleman wrote in a rage, informing his self-expatriating son that if he chose to neglect his profession and waste his time upon the banks of the Nile, he might make up his mind to live upon the backsheesh of his fellow pilgrims; for not one English shilling would ever be remitted in that direction.

"Now," resumed Helen, "I find that I must have another bridesmaid. Mr. Petersfeld is engaged to be married to a Miss Linda Buttermere; and if you take the one, I mean to lay claim to the other. Could it possibly be managed, do you think? Ferdinand, you must really contrive it!"

"That I will, darling! My father will be only too delighted with such an opportunity of firing off his diplomacy. Nothing on earth will please him more than to be told that it is your wish, but that we fear the thing is impossible! Hey? Can't you fancy the grave twinkle in his eye, and the tone with which he will repeat the last word? It will be a whole day's employ- ment to consider the proper scheme, arrange the exact means, and write the necessary despatches. And the best of it is, that he will succeed. You'll see!"

"It will really be great fun!"

"It will be a piece of luck, too, for Miss Linda," laughed Ferdinand. "What do you think that same prodigal father did when I went up to town the other day? Abso- lutely gave me three hundred pounds to lay out upon lockets for the bridesmaids! They are, of course, all alike, with our initials intertwisted in brilliants. I think you will be pleased with the monogram."

"Three hundred pounds! I never heard of such a thing."

"O, and I forgot to tell you that the Gigoggin business is settled at last. The Admiral has given way, and allows him to follow you. I suppose my father was right in insisting upon a regular written character, just as if old Gi had been a perfect stranger. Like Salterton, he has a strong feeling about what he calls tampering with other people's retainers. However, all is right now. Your henchman is again in your service."

"What! Another piece of good fortune! O, Ferdinand how very kind you all are. I don't know how I should have managed without Gi."

"I say much the same, for my own part. In fact, I'm not so certain that I should have been where I am without him," rejoined Ferdinand, gaily. "He won't find me ungrateful. He is a made man for life."

The wedding was a brilliant affair. It took place of course at Riverwood. I am not ashamed to confess that few things would amuse me more than to read a circumstantial account of it written by a snob.

"And so," said Mr. Salterton, as Helen appeared at their early breakfast-table on the morning of the eventful day, "I find that Lord St. Margarets has been considerate enough to provide me with an accomplice upon this occasion. I suppose he thought the knot would be all the tighter for a pull at both ends."

"Indeed!" replied Helen, who felt just nervous enough to be glad of an indifferent matter to talk about. "One of his friends, I suppose."

"I expect him here presently. He said he should ride over from Saintswood. He is a man whom I remember well at Oxford, and hadn't seen for years until yesterday. And here he comes, I believe."

There was a clatter of horse-hoofs along the approach, and then a rattling ring at the front-door bell.

The door opened, and the visitor was announced.

"Doctor Orchard, sir."

"Ha! my dear Miss Fleetlands! You told me that we should meet again; but you didn't tell me how very soon it was to be. That was inconsiderate. I must have a kiss for my journey; and here are a thousand good wishes in advance of to-day's business. Mrs. Orchard sends the same. So does my sister. Three thousand in all! My dear young lady, how shall I ever thank you enough for coming to my house?"

"How can I ever thank you enough for coming here to-day," returned Helen, ready to cry with pleasure. "Do you know, Doctor Orchard, I scarcely felt as if my happiness could have been added to; but you have made it really run over."

"O dear me! If we are to compliment each other at this rate, we shall certainly be late for church. The good fortune is all upon my part. Your gallant young bridegroom was kind enough to write to me the other day, and offer me his father's hospitality at Saintswood for the wedding, in case I could manage to come and lend a hand. What a princely place it is! Long and happily may you live to reign over it. And now Helen," continued the Doctor, taking her once more by the hand—"I'm always going to call you Helen, in future, you know —I congratulate you in earnest. You have chosen well. There is no mistake about it. That cross was not won by vulgar muscle, nor by blind carelessness of danger, nor by the instinct which makes all true men happy to fight. That glorious cross fell to a man whom God had fashioned as one fit to win and wear it; and if that young fellow had touched his hat to me at a stable-door, I should have taken off mine to him in return. I should indeed. To mistake that face would be to insult its maker. You are a heretic as to all this, Salterton?"

"Open to conviction; sine comburendo, if possible. Not, I confess, upon the strength of two individual instances, and those two—Helen and Ferdinand.

Doctor Orchard ought to have made his bargain for at least ten more kisses before Helen retired to her bridal toilette. He had indeed made her love him dearly.

Of the wedding itself, one or two incidents are all that I feel it at all desirable to record. In the first place the Admiral made his appearance, in accordance with a formal invitation. He shook hands cordially with Lord St. Margarets', as well as with the bride and bridegroom ; and went home with a lighter heart than he had carried for some years before.

Linda was not present. Diplomacy had done its best; but had failed upon this occasion. Shortly after the ceremony, Petersfeld found an opportunity of approaching Helen.

"You must let me offer you this little talisman, Mrs. Hunsdon," he said, "with my warmest congratulations and good wishes. Will you wear it sometimes for my sake. I brought it from Egypt. We

can never be quite indifferent to each other,
I hope."

"Indeed, we cannot, Mr. Petersfeld,"
replied Helen, admiring the sparkling toy.
"Thank you very much indeed. Did it
really come from Egypt? It shall always
have a place on my chain. It is a talisman
for good I hope :—but I am so sorry that
Linda could not be here."

"Come, Helen, we mustn't ask questions," said Captain Hunsdon, approaching.
"Petersfeld and I had a conversation last
evening ; but never mind that now. Petersfeld, I am going to give you a commission.
—Will you undertake it ?"

"With pleasure."

"It is to convey this bridesmaid-locket to
Miss Buttermere. I trust to your honour
to present it personally. You will tell her,

please, how grieved we all were that she was unable to be present, to wear it in her place."

"And tell her, from me," added Helen, "that I hope she will be as much in love with her talisman as I am with mine."

"Must I really——" began Petersfeld.

"Certainly. It is in your charge."

There was no time for more. There is not much opportunity for private conversation upon these occasions.

"Then I will carry it."

Petersfeld kept his promise like a man. But I shall not tell you what passed at the interview. I have special reasons for this reservation. Whether or not, to use ladies' language, 'anything came of it,' every lady in the land is at liberty to conjecture for herself. And the lady who guesses right will have read my story to greater advantage than the lady who guesses wrong.

THE END.

BILLING, PRINTER, GUILDFORD.

www.ingramcontent.com/pod-product-compliance
Lightning Source LLC
Chambersburg PA
CBHW020844020726

47497CB00005B/1255